Beaten and unwanted by her insane mother, Lori ran away from home one night to try and live the way she felt like living. Out of money and not sure which way to turn, a man named Lawrence took her under his wing and provided for her—but it was a high price she had to pay for security. Caught in the world of prostitution, it looked as though she might never be able to leave the life of streetwalking behind her. Then Rich Whitmore stepped into her life—was he the way out? Find out how a reckless chase scene almost ended her life, but ended up turning her life of misery into one of meaning and direction.

More Outstanding Books by John Benton

☐	Carmen	$3.50
☐	Patti	$3.50
☐	Lefty	$3.50
☐	Lori	$3.50
☐	Sherri	$3.50
☐	Kari	$3.50
☐	Terri	$3.50
☐	Debbie	$3.50
☐	Sheila	$3.50
☐	Jackie	$3.50

Buy them at your local Christian book store or use this handy coupon for ordering:

LORI

John Benton

John Benton Books
Box 94304
218 So. Madison
Pasadena, CA 91109

Scripture quotations in this volume are from the King James Version of the Bible.

Library of Congress Cataloging in Publication Data

Benton, John, date
   Lori.

   I. Title.
PZ4.B4788Lo   [PS3552.E57]   813′.54   80-10139
ISBN 0-8007-8385-9

TO
my friend Frances Wingate,
whose vital faith
and overwhelming enthusiasm
always lift the fallen.

Garrison, NY   Pasadena, CA

ONE

"Lori!" my mother screamed. "Slow down! You'll kill us both!"

I acted as if I were stone-deaf. I just gritted my teeth and floored the accelerator. The car lunged forward.

"Did you hear me? I said slow down, young lady, or you're going to get yourself into real trouble!"

I glanced at the speedometer. Seventy-five! A little bit more, and I'd have it up to eighty!

Out of the corner of my eye I could see Mother stiffening. Inside I laughed. Finally I was getting to her!

"Lori!" she screamed again—this time more in panic than anger. "Stop this car right now! Do you hear me?"

"Say a prayer, Mother," I said mockingly. "This is it!"

"No! No!" she yelled. "Look out for that truck!"

I saw it just ahead, and beyond that the curve. Either I had to take my chances of passing in a no-passing zone or of slamming into the rear of that semi. Mother grabbed for the wheel, but I slapped her hand away.

"I'm going to kill myself!" I yelled.

"Don't! No, Lori, don't! Don't do such a foolish thing!"

With that she lunged forward, putting her head between her knees and sobbing hysterically.

I waited until the last possible moment, and then I hit the brakes hard. She heard the wheels screeching and groaned, bracing herself for the crash she knew was coming.

When she felt the car slowing and nothing else happening, she looked up, her face drawn and pale. Her bony finger pointed at my face. "Lori," she shouted, "that was the most stupid thing you've ever done. What on earth came over you?"

I hee-hawed. "Oh, Mom, it was all a big joke. What's the matter? Can't you take a joke? Do you think I really want to kill myself?"

"Well, I really don't care if you want to kill yourself," she replied. "I just don't want to be around when you do it! And no, I don't think it's funny. You won't, either, when your father gets home tonight! He's going to ground you!"

I could live through being grounded. But didn't my mother really care whether I lived or died?

I didn't have much time to think about that because just then I heard a siren, right behind me, and saw a red light flashing—state police!

Now I stopped.

"You stupid, stupid kid," mother berated me. "You're going to get a ticket. Serves you right."

"Yes," I responded. "Maybe I'll even get my license suspended. Then who will drive you around on all your stupid errands?"

"Oh, no! Lori, we've got to think of something!"

We didn't have time to think because the officer was already standing alongside my window. I rolled it down, all the while trying to look as penitent as possible.

"Ma'am, may I see your operator's license?"

I fumbled in my purse and finally located it.

As he took it, he studied it carefully. Then he looked back at me. "Now tell me, young lady, where were you going in such a big hurry?"

Before I could even open my mouth, Mother answered, "You see, officer, we were in a hurry to get back home. My sister, Lori's aunt, is quite ill at our house. She ran out of her medicine, so we went to get some. She's supposed to have it within ten minutes. I guess this whole thing is my fault. I've been so nervous about my sister's illness. I was rushing Lori and didn't realize she was speeding. I'm terribly sorry."

"Officer," I interrupted, "that's a dirty lie. I was speeding because I was trying to kill myself."

"Well, well! this is all very interesting. But which one of you is telling me the truth?"

"I am!" we both said.

"Officer, don't you believe that little smart aleck," Mother said as convincingly as she could. "She's a filthy liar!"

"Mother, how dare you talk that way? I know the law, and when you talk to the law, you've got to tell the truth. Now, sir, believe me. I picked out that truck, and I was going to kill myself. I want to die. I don't care what my old lady says. I wanted to die!"

Mother dug her fingernails into my arm "Lori!" she screamed. "You tell the man the truth!"

I wrenched free. "No, Mother! *You* tell the truth!"

She started to grab my hair, but the officer barked, "Stop it, you two! I don't know what's going on here, but there's no sense coming to blows about it! Now simmer down, or I'll arrest both of you!"

That scared Mother. She pulled her hand back and stiffened into the seat.

"Okay, young lady, you'd better come back to my car."

He put me in the backseat of the patrol car, and he got into the front. Still looking at my license he picked up his radio and called in my number. I guess he was checking it out to be sure it was legal. It was.

He shifted his huge frame to face me. "Now let's go over this once more. Were you on your way to help your aunt, or were you trying to kill yourself?"

"Neither."

"Okay, then; what gives?"

"Actually we were just going home from the grocery store. Mom can't drive, so I have to take her on her stupid errands. I don't even have an aunt living in New York."

"And what about you? Were you trying to commit suicide?"

I laughed. "No, not really, officer. I just wanted to scare my old lady. Honestly, I don't know what came over me, but I thought that for once I would try to call her bluff. I guess I wanted to know if she really cared if I lived or died. And would you believe she was screaming only about herself? She said she didn't care if I died. But, no, I really didn't intend to kill myself."

"I guess you know you did a very stupid thing. I was waiting for speeding violators back there when you went sailing by at seventy. I took out after you. Then I saw that curve up ahead and that truck. I knew I couldn't get to you in time. So when I saw your brake lights, I breathed a deep sigh of relief.

"If you're going to try to kill yourself, don't do it in an automobile. Sometimes it doesn't work."

"What do you mean, it doesn't work? If I had hit that truck, it would have been curtains!"

"Probably. But sometimes people live through

accidents such as that. The tragic part is that they're half-dead. Sometimes they're paralyzed from the waist down; sometimes they're blinded; sometimes they lose an arm or a leg. Believe me, for some of them, it's almost worse living!"

"You mean people really do try to kill themselves with cars?"

"Not usually. I suppose maybe a few try it, but I don't think it's the usual way."

"Tell me something, officer," I said as I leaned toward him. "Something's been bothering me ever since I learned to drive."

"What's that?"

"Well, as I have been driving down the highway by myself, I sometimes get this funny urge that maybe I should swing into an oncoming car, hit it head-on, and kill myself. In fact, just last week I had that crazy urge and had to grip the steering wheel to keep from doing it. It scared me half to death. I mean this is really bothering me. Do you think it means I'll do it someday?"

He laughed. I didn't think it was funny!

"Well, young lady, let me tell you something about that phenomenon. Most people experience it at some time or other, and it is really strange. I have had hundreds of people ask me about it. You know something else? I even feel that way myself! But it's rarely anything more than a fleeting thought. It's just a strange thing about life. As long as you keep your head, it won't happen to you—or to me."

"Really?"

"Honest, that's the truth. It's a very common feeling. Don't let it worry you."

"Well, that certainly relieves my mind."

"Good. But, young lady, I must tell you one more thing before I let you go. I really should give you a ticket, but I'm going to give you a break. I see that you and your mother aren't getting along well. It's quite evident."

"You can say that again! I'm really having a tough time with that woman."

"Well, don't be too hard on your mother. Moms and dads are frustrated today about how to raise kids. I ought to know. I've got six of them at home!"

"Have you got a daughter like me?"

"I kind of think so. She's fifteen; I see you're seventeen. We have our disagreements, of course. But all in all she's been a good daughter."

"She's really lucky to have you for a father."

"Well, you know, you have to work at it."

"Officer, you're such a nice man. Why don't you just adopt me?"

"I'll tell you what. After I raise my own kids, then maybe I can adopt you. Maybe we could get along, then."

We both laughed.

"Okay," he said, "as I told you, I'm going to give you a break. But you've got to promise me you'll never try anything like this again. If I catch you speeding, it's going to be a ticket. You'll probably lose your license. Do you understand?"

"Yes, sir! You have my word. I'll never do anything that stupid ever again!"

When I got back to our car, Mother was ready to start in on me. She had been sitting there seething all that time.

"Hey, wait, Mother. Don't say one little word. You open your mouth, and it starts all over again. That cop is still sitting back there. I got away with it. So keep your mouth shut and let's get out of here."

"You little guttersnipe," she exploded. "Don't you

even think of trying to pull something like that again!"

"Mom, like I told you, keep your mouth shut. I admitted to the officer that I was the one who lied. I told him we really did need to get the medicine to my aunt right away. So I've got to get out of here quick. If he hears you screaming, he'll be right back up here. And then we'll both be in big trouble!"

I knew I had to lie. My mother sometimes had fits of rage. I couldn't afford having her upset now and blowing the whole thing. Maybe letting her have her so-called way would cool her down.

I guess it worked. She stared straight ahead as I started the car and eased out into traffic. In fact, my threat worked so well that she didn't say one word all the way home. And that worried me.

We lived in Queens, New York—on a peaceful street where the neighbors got along with each other pretty well. I just wished my folks and I had peace within the four walls of our home. It seemed that every minute was a hassle about something.

My father travels—he's a salesman. He was home more now, but I could remember when I was little that he used to be gone for months at a time.

I didn't know much about Dad's side of the family. I knew Mother had a sister in Florida and another one in Illinois. But we never heard from them. My grandparents lived on the West Coast. I'd never seen them.

As we drove up to our house, my sister, Peggy, was just getting home from somewhere. She was thirteen and had her head screwed on right. In spite of our squabbles, I really liked her. We could stick together through family conflicts.

Peggy helped carry the groceries in and set them in the kitchen. Mother didn't lift a finger. All she did was gripe about how much it cost to feed a family.

For me it was a godsend that Peggy came home. She could help me stand up to Mother.

Then it came. "Lori, come into the bedroom a minute," Mother commanded.

Peggy looked at her quizzically. "Peggy, I want you to leave the house for about fifteen minutes. I've got something I want to talk to Lori about privately."

"Oh, Mom. I wanted to watch a TV program and—"

"Don't 'Oh, Mom' me, young lady. I said for you to leave this house for fifteen minutes, and I mean it!"

Detecting the rising anger in Mother's voice, Peggy headed for the front door.

I heard the front door slam. This was going to be it.

Mother grabbed my arm and pulled me into her bedroom. Her fists were clenched, her face drained of color.

"Come on, Mom. I know you're upset, but it wasn't all that bad. I didn't get any ticket. Nothing happened."

She glared at me, her nose just inches away from mine. "Lori, I have never been so humiliated in all my life! There I was, trying to help you avoid getting a ticket, and you made up that filthy lie about wanting to commit suicide!"

I backed away slightly. "Mother, it wasn't a lie," I said as calmly as I could. "I'm sick and tired of this life. I really did have an urge to kill myself. The only thing that stopped me was that I didn't want you to get hurt."

"That's another filthy lie!" she yelled. "You're too chicken to commit suicide. You were just smarting off, trying to make me look bad to that officer."

"Okay, Mom. Have it your way. I'm sorry."

"What do you mean, you're sorry? You think that takes care of everything, don't you? Well, let me tell you something. Do you know who that man was? He lives on the other side of town, but I know his wife. He'll go home and tell her what happened, and then she'll spread it all over this community. Because of your dirty lies, they're going to start spreading around that I told a lie."

"Well, you did tell one, didn't you?"

I shouldn't have said that. Her hand stung my face before I could protect myself. I fell back, grabbed my jaw, and yelled, "Why are you slapping me?"

"Because you need to be slapped, you little fool!"

I pulled myself up to my full five feet four inches, put my nose practically against hers, and shouted, "Don't you ever slap me again!"

Smack! She hit me harder this time. I reeled across the room like a drunk and slumped against the wall. I sat there rubbing my jaw for a few moments and slowly got to my feet.

"I don't think you understood, Mother. I said, 'Don't you ever slap me again!'"

This time I saw her hand coming and ducked. That really aggravated her.

I could taste the blood seeping from the corner of my mouth. My lip started to swell. *Won't I be a pretty sight now!* I thought.

That's when I lost control and cursed her repeatedly. She lunged and grabbed my hair. Yanking on it, she pushed me and pulled me toward the wall. The next thing I knew, she started beating my head against the wall unmercifully.

I kept up the screaming and cursing. Oh, how I wanted to slap her back, but somehow I just couldn't bring myself to hit my own mother.

The furniture began going around in circles, and I slumped to the floor.

When I came to, my head throbbed as though a thousand jackhammers were pounding inside. Mother stood over me, looking like an escapee from the insane asylum.

"Now maybe that will teach you a lesson, young lady. If we ever get stopped by a policeman again, you go along with what I say. Don't you ever embarrass me again. Do you understand?"

From my position on the floor Mother seemed to be twenty feet tall. And she looked like the devil.

"Okay, you win. I'll never do that again."

"That's better. Now get up. You're lucky I didn't kill you."

"Thanks," I sneered.

I hobbled into the bathroom to see how much damage she had done to me. My face was swollen. Black and blue marks were starting to show on my forehead. I started wiping the blood off my mouth. *Ouch! That smarts!*

In the corner of the mirror I could see my mother in the doorway. Was that crazy woman going to start in on me again—or had she come to rejoice in the damages?

Why was something like this happening to me? Why couldn't I have been born into another home, a happy home, maybe like that police officer's home. I'll bet he didn't beat his children! My pent-up anger let loose in a torrent of tears.

"Now stop your crying, little baby," Mother taunted. "You'll be as good as new in a day or two."

"Mother," I sobbed, "what will I tell my friends— that you beat me up?"

She elbowed her way in and grabbed my chin.

"Mother, please! Please! Don't hit me again! Don't hit me again!"

"I will hit you again whenever I happen to feel like it. So shut up and listen. This is what I want you to tell, and you'd better get it straight. You tell your friends you fell down the basement stairs. You banged your lips and your head on the steps as you were falling, and when you got to the bottom, you were unconscious. Do you understand that?"

I nodded. Another lie. Mother was always lying. Come to think of it, so was I. Maybe that's why it was so easy for me—because it was easy for her. Would I be like her in other ways, too? Would I beat my children? I shuddered at that idea!

I heard the front door slam. Peggy! She would be looking for me. She'd want to know what Mother had had to say.

When she got to the bathroom door and saw me, she screamed, "Lori! What in the world happened to you?"

Oh, how I wanted to tell the truth for once. But just then Mother walked up behind her.

"Oh, nothing, really," I said as nonchalantly as I could. "Clumsy me. I was taking some dirty clothes to the basement and I tripped. I guess I must have bounced along and been knocked out. When I came to, Mother was bent over me crying her eyes out. She thought maybe I had died or something."

Mother still had that sneer on her face, but I could tell she was pleased with the way I had handled her story. As far as she was concerned, everything was okay now.

But Peggy had another idea. "Lori, you look terrible. I think we'd better take you down to the hospital. You may have some broken bones or something."

Great idea, kid! Then maybe there would be an investigation. Those people see child-beating cases all the time. They could tell I hadn't fallen down any steps.

Child-beating. I'd sure like to pin that rap on my old lady!

"Oh, no! No!" Mother interrupted. "Nothing like that needs to be done, Peggy."

Peggy looked at her suspiciously.

"I've checked Lori over thoroughly, Peggy. She just has a few bruises and a split lip. It'll heal in a day or so.

"Besides," she went on, "we just can't afford any more expenses right now. You know if she goes to the hospital, they'll run all sorts of tests and take X rays. They'll probably put her in the hospital for a week. We can take better care of her right here. Can't we, Lori?"

"Yes," I mumbled. "I feel okay. Just a couple of scratches and bumps, that's all. No big deal. No need to waste money on doctors and hospitals. I'll live."

"Well, I think you should see a doctor. You look as if you've been in a fifteen-round fight."

Did Peggy suspect what had happened?

"Now, Peggy, don't make it any worse than it is—just a few little scratches. I'll be okay."

I gently pushed her out of the bathroom and locked the door. Emotionally drained, I crumpled to the floor, put my face between my knees, and sobbed as though my world had come to an end.

What was life all about, anyway? Maybe I really should commit suicide. Mother wouldn't care. Maybe life wasn't worth living, anyway. Why tough it out? And if I killed myself, maybe the world would get to see what a horrible mother I had!

There must be some way I could take my life—some way that wouldn't leave me a mangled cripple instead of dead.

My mind was still foggy from the beating, but suddenly I thought of something. Why not? I knew it would work. But I needed help. If I could just get Peggy to help me.

TWO

Supper that night was dreadfully quiet. Father attended a Lions' Club dinner, so the three of us didn't talk much. Every bite I took hurt, and I finally just pushed my plate back and left the table.

Peggy and I still had to do the dishes. Mother went in and watched TV. Now for my plan. . . .

"Peggy," I lied, "I just don't know what I'm going to do. This pain is so severe that I'm ready to blow my brains out." I put down the towel and dropped into a kitchen chair.

Peggy dried her hands, came over, and put her arm around me. "You poor dear! I know how you must be suffering. You do look a little better, but I know you must be hurting. Is there anything I can get you?"

This was going to be easier than I had thought.

"I hate to trouble you, but, yes, there is. If I had some of those prescription painkillers, they would take care of me."

"Hey, that's a smart idea! Why didn't I think of that?"

"Well, I really don't like to take anything that strong, but I've got to do something. I think maybe my cheekbone is fractured. How does it look to you?"

She reached toward it, and I drew back.

"No! No! Don't touch me, Peggy. I couldn't bear it!"

"Oh, sorry!" She leaned back, carefully scrutinizing every detail of my face.

"Well, I can't see anything, but it is awfully banged up. Maybe it *is* broken."

"Well, if I could just get some of those painkillers, I'm sure I would be all right."

"No problem, Lori. I'll walk you down to the hospital emergency room."

"Come on, Peggy. You know we just can't walk in there and ask for painkillers. The kind of painkillers I need have to come from a doctor, and a doctor will insist on examining me—and that will cost a bundle. You heard Mom. We can't afford anything like that."

"I guess I was just remembering what happened to me," she responded. "Remember a couple of years ago when a car hit me as I was riding my bicycle? I wasn't hurt all that much, but they rushed me to the emergency room. My legs were really hurting. I remember the doctor gave me some yellow and pink pills for the pain."

"That's what I need—those yellow pills!"

"Then you'll have to go to the hospital."

"No! No! We can't do that! I'd have to stay a whole week. Remember?"

Silence.

"I know where I can get some of those painkillers," I announced.

"Where?"

"At the drugstore."

"Of course!" Peggy responded. "I'll go right now and get some."

"One problem, Peggy."

"What's that?"

"You don't have a doctor's prescription."

"Oh."

"But there's a solution to that."

"There is? Oh, Lori, no! You won't forge a—"

"No way! Nothing like that, little sister. I have another idea."

"Like what?"

"Like trust me. It's simple. But I'll have to go with you."

"You feel like going out?"

"Peggy, I'll do anything to get rid of this pain!"

"Okay, Lori, I'm game. Let's go."

She yelled to Mom that we were going down to the drugstore to see what was happening. Mom didn't respond. She resented any intrusion when she was watching TV. I guess she was glad we were going.

As we walked along, Peggy said, "Okay now; what gives?"

"Peggy, this may sound stupid at first, but here's what we'll do."

She looked at me intently.

"When we get into that drugstore, I'm going to strip."

"You're going to do what?" she shrieked.

"I'm going to take off my clothes in that drugstore!"

"Come off it, Lori. Streaking went out years ago. Besides, how's a stupid thing like that going to get any painkillers for you?"

"I'm getting to that. Everyone in that drugstore will stop and watch a naked girl running around. I'll guarantee you that. If there are any old men in the store, they'll hoot and holler in delight. It's really going to be funny!"

"Funny? I think it's disgusting and stupid. I'd never take off my clothes in public."

"Well, little sister, you don't have much to show

anyway! But what I've got will attract some attention!"

"Listen, Lori, I'm not having anything to do with your stupid idea. I'm going back home. You go on down to the drugstore and streak if you want to. Not me!"

She turned in disgust.

"Wait, Peggy! Don't go back on me now. This pain is really killing me. I need help!"

"Yes, you need help. I know that. But I can't see what streaking's got to do with painkillers. I just can't see it."

"I'm coming to that, Peggy. While I'm streaking, all you have to do is jump behind the counter, grab a couple of bottles of those painkillers, and we're on our way. Believe me, nobody will see you take them. They'll all be watching me!"

Peggy just stood there, her mouth opening slowly to echo her shock. "Lori, so help me, I can't believe you would stoop to something like this! Absolutely, I mean absolutely, no way am I going to steal painkillers!"

"Oh, Peggy, don't be that way. I'll tell you what, then. You do the stripping, and I'll do the stealing."

"Are you kidding? You already said I don't have anything to show. Besides, I couldn't do that. You must be crazy, Lori."

"Not crazy," I answered softly. "Desperate."

I let that sink in.

"Okay, Peggy, you leave me no choice. I'm heading for the hospital. I know Dad will be furious over the bills, but I've got to get some relief."

I headed toward the hospital, hoping that Peggy would call my bluff. Sure enough, I hadn't gone far when I heard footsteps behind me.

"Lori, wait a minute. Let's discuss this again. There's got to be some way we can get you those painkillers without your streaking and my stealing."

"I can't come up with any other way," I told her. "I

don't have a prescription to forge. I hate to go to the hospital and make Dad pay all those bills unnecessarily. This is the only way to do it."

"Your way is stupid, Lori. Come on. I'm going to the hospital with you. Dad will understand."

Wrong reaction! Somehow I had to stop her!

"Peggy, I've got to level with you. See these bruises? See this mutilated face? The pain is killing me. Do you know how it happened?"

"Sure. You said you fell down the basement stairs."

"That was a lie, Peggy. Mother beat me up."

She looked at me incredulously.

"Why do you think she told you to get out of the house? So she could beat me up. I pulled a little scheme in the car about committing suicide and scared her. Then we got into a ruckus with a state cop. Mother came home with great vengeance. I knew I was going to get it, but I didn't think she'd stoop to beating me up this way. I know it's hard to believe she could do something like this, but so help me, it's the truth. I'm not lying to you."

Peggy stared at the ground and then started to cry.

"What's the matter?"

"Nothing. Nothing."

"Now don't just stand there and tell me 'nothing.' Something's bugging you, and it's not my problem. What is it?"

"Well, if I tell you, promise never to tell?"

"Listen, you're my sister. I promise that to my dying day I'll never breathe a word."

"Remember that bicycle accident when I had to go to the hospital? Remember how badly bruised my legs were? Well, it wasn't any accident. I had stolen a cigarette from Mother, and she found out. She flew into a rage, took a stick, and beat me on the legs until the blood flowed. Then she told me to make up a big story about an accident."

So that was it. Mother had beaten up Peggy, too!

"Oh, wow! We really have a problem on our hands, don't we? I think it's time someone gave her a good working over."

"Oh, no, Lori. We should never do anything like that!" She was probably right. Mother must have a sick mind. Beating on her wouldn't help.

"When Mother took me to the hospital," Peggy continued, "they did give me those painkillers. But from the questions they asked, I think they suspected something. Anyway, when we got home, Mother got out my bicycle and ran the car over it—just to make her story stick! I was furious! It was just about all I could take."

"So we both have scars from the great battle. But I still don't think the hospital's a good idea. They'd ask a lot of questions, and our family's name would be in the papers. If the cops started asking about what happened, I'd have to tell the truth. You know that, don't you?"

She nodded.

"Okay, Peggy, what about the little drugstore caper? Does it sound better now?"

"Not really, but I'm mad enough to go along. You'd just better be sure it works!"

"Not to worry, kid!" I slapped her on the back. "We could do great as partners in crime."

"Stop kidding about it, Lori. I'm only doing this to help you get relief. Believe me, if there were any other way...."

"There's no other way, Peggy."

We walked the rest of the way in silence.

At the entrance to the drugstore we stopped and

peeked in. About five people were inside. The druggist was busy at the counter, just as I had hoped he would be. Everything was go.

"Now remember," I whispered, "I'll try to keep my face covered. But when I take off my clothes, I'll start running through the store. Sure as anything, that druggist will try to catch me. When he does and when everybody's watching me, you just jump behind that counter, find some yellow jackets, and take off. I'll meet you back at the house. You go in first, but try not to let the druggist see you."

"How will you keep your face covered?"

"I'm way ahead of you, kid. Here—I've got this ski mask in my pocket. Help me. Ouch! Careful!"

Peggy walked in, and I waited. I even unbuttoned my blouse outside—so I wouldn't lose my nerve, I guess. I wondered if it was worth all this hassle.

My heart pounding, I entered the drugstore. Nobody was watching yet. I slipped off my blouse, then my jeans. My heart started beating so wildly that I thought I would pass out. This was so embarrassing!

I jerked off my underclothes and took off down an aisle.

First I heard a woman scream. She headed for the door. I ran by the counter. The druggist's mouth flew open in disbelief, and he started chasing me, yelling at the top of his voice. I simply ran down another aisle shouting, "Yippee! Yippee! Yippee!"

That attracted everybody's attention, and the chase was on! I headed down another aisle and caught a glimpse of Peggy behind the counter. So far, so good.

Now for the door. Oh, no! Standing smack in front of the door stood a huge man, his arms stretched out to catch me.

I guess I surprised him when I stopped just before I

got to him and picked up my clothes. Then as he reached two big hands toward me, I shouted, "Don't touch me, or you'll be arrested for molesting a girl!"

He jerked back so fast that even I was surprised. You should have seen his face. Oh, that was hilarious!

I took off down the street. One guy started clapping and cheering. And somebody was still chasing me.

Brakes screeched. A guy poked his head out of the car window and yelled, "Hey, baby, whatever you're doing, I'll be glad to help you out!"

I ran the other way. I certainly didn't want to jump into any car with a stranger!

By the sound of it, there must be three men chasing me now. I had to get out of this situation—fast.

Up ahead I spotted a group of young boys. They saw me, too—and had formed a half-circle to grab me when I ran by. I couldn't have that.

I started across the street, and a car headed right for me. It looked like a woman driving—and she was by herself. I jumped out into the middle of her lane and held my hands up high. She slammed on the brakes. I jumped in with her and screamed, "Quick! Get out of here! They're after me!"

Without a word she pushed the accelerator to the floorboard, and we peeled rubber. The light ahead was red, but she laid on the horn and we sailed right on through!

She drove on frantically, her mouth wide open, too scared to say a word.

Six blocks later I ordered her to turn left. She wheeled it around the corner. Then I said, "Stop!"

She slammed on the brakes. I jumped out and ran between two houses. I heard her take off.

Poor woman. She had reacted so strangely. Probably

she'd been raped or had gotten into something serious and was reliving her past. But she hadn't said one word.

I pulled my clothes on quickly, but I was still winded from all that running. I sat there and rested a few minutes before I walked the remaining two blocks to my home.

When I walked in, Peggy was on the sofa, her head in her hands. Mother glared at me.

"Lori, so help me, I don't know what I'm going to have to do with you. I feel like killing you with my bare hands!"

"Hey, just cool it!" I shot back. "What are you yelling about?"

"You know very well what I'm yelling about! The very idea of you streaking at the drugstore! I'm so embarrassed!"

"Whatever are you talking about? I didn't do any streaking! Who told you a lie like that?"

I glanced at Peggy. She must have told.

"Mrs. Hattle just called me. She was in the drugstore and she recognized you—even with that ski mask on!"

"Oh, come on, Mom; it was just a little joke. I had a lot of fun, and I didn't hurt anybody. I mean I didn't do anything to anybody. I didn't steal anything. It was just for laughs. I thought it was really funny."

"Well, I don't think it was funny!"

"Oh, come on. Can't you take a little joke?"

She started toward me, her eyes on fire. I knew what she had in mind. But no way was I going to take another beating.

She lunged. I stepped aside, and she lost her balance. I threw my arms around her neck and pushed her hard to the floor. Her hands and feet were going in every direction. I dropped onto her, squeezed my fingers around her neck, and screamed, "Mother, stop! If you open your mouth or lay a hand on me, I'm going to tell everybody how you beat me!"

"That's a lie!" she screamed. "That's a dirty, filthy lie! I've never beaten you in my life!"

I tightened my grip around her neck. "So you think it's a lie. Well, I'll tell you something. I know about what you did to Peggy two years ago. She knows what you did to me today. If you don't cool it right now, we're heading down to the police station to have you arrested for child abuse. You'll go to jail. Do you hear me?"

I felt her body relax. Her hands fell slowly to her sides, and she let her feet and legs out straight. I released my grip. I knew she had gotten the message.

Slowly I pushed my way up and sat in a chair, watching her. She stayed there silently—no movement, no talking. Her labored breathing was the only evidence of our struggle.

Peggy hadn't moved the whole time, either. She was still staring at the floor, transfixed.

Mother slowly rolled over, got to her knees, and stumbled to the big chair, avoiding my gaze—and still totally silent.

"Peggy," I said, "I want to see you in the bedroom for a minute."

Mother didn't make a move to stop us.

As I shut the door of the bedroom, I whispered, "Did you get those pain pills?"

"Lori, do you think you should have told Mother? Should you have threatened her?"

"Never mind about that, Peggy. That's done with. Did you get those pills?"

A big grin crossed her face. "Sure did!" she said proudly. "It was easy. They were right in front."

She reached into her pocket and pulled out a nice, big bottle of yellow jackets.

"Lori, I must tell you something. You really did look funny tearing around that drugstore with only a ski mask on. I couldn't believe my eyes. You should have seen those two old men who were in the store, and even the druggist. After you had run out the front door, they were all laughing and slapping their knees. To them it was the best show in town!"

I laughed. Maybe I had livened up our neighborhood a little. But that really didn't matter to me now. I had something else in mind.

Pills in hand, I headed for the bathroom. I was going to get even with my mother this time!

THREE

Quickly I popped a couple of the yellow jackets. I felt a tingling way down in my stomach. So this was what it felt like. Good! I'd pop a couple more!

Yes, I really was going to show my mother. If it embarrassed her for me to streak, what would she say when I became a junkie? That should really start her friends talking!

Pills were the way to start, I decided. Then heroin. That kind of fix would really fix her!

No way in the world was my mother going to beat me and get away with it. No, I probably never would go to the authorities. But now that I knew she'd hurt both Peggy and me, I was going to teach her a lesson. The whole neighborhood would know that Mrs. Hutton's daughter Lori was a good-for-nothing junkie. I thought of her embarrassment and laughed aloud. The old phony!

The tingling in my stomach started moving into other parts of my body. Why not try some more? Another pill. Another gulp of water.

I leaned against the sink, half-giddy and staring into

the mirror. The tingling moved down my arms and legs. Nothing really seemed to matter except the feeling. Reality sort of faded away. I popped another pill and swallowed hard. Then another. And another. And another.

I reached for another, and that's the last thing I remember.

My eyes! I can't open them! My eyelids must be made of lead.

My hands! Why can't I lift them? Why can't I make them move?

With great effort I opened my eyes and tried to look around. The strain almost killed me—it hurt so much. All I could see was white.

My eyes closed effortlessly. Could I open them again? Once more I struggled. This time vision became clearer. I could make out the features of my mother's face.

"Get away from me!" I yelled. "Get out of here. You have no right to come into the bathroom when I'm using it! Get out of here, now!"

"Lori, darling, don't you know where you are?"

Where was I? In bed? Strange. This wasn't my room. The bathroom wasn't big enough for a bed. *My arms. Something . . .* My eyes followed the tubes from my arms to the overhead intravenous bottles. Then it hit me: *hospital!*

"What am I doing here? Who brought me here? Why. . . ."

"Hold on, Lori. One question at a time. I brought you here. Young lady, don't you realize I saved your life? You were out cold in that bathroom, and Peggy and I rushed you here. You'd better thank your lucky stars that I'm the one who saved you from dying of an overdose!"

"What do you mean, overdose? I'm no junkie. You won't find any needle marks on my arms."

"Stop playing your little games, Lori. Two days ago you stole that bottle of pills from the drugstore. You'd better change your ways pretty quickly because there's lots of trouble ahead for you!"

"What do you mean, two days ago? I just got here, didn't I?"

Mother laughed hollowly. "I mean two days ago, Lori. You've been out for two days, and the doctors and nurses have been working feverishly to keep you alive. Twice they thought your heart had stopped. You came so close to death's door that you should have seen what it looks like open!"

"Oh, get off it. I wish I were dead, anyway."

She raised her hand as though she were going to strike me in the face.

"Mom, don't!" I yelled with what little energy I could muster. "Don't do a stupid thing like that—especially not in the hospital! You'll be arrested for sure!"

I guess that stopped her. She moved away, toward the window.

She should be the one in this hospital bed, I decided. She was so sick that the least little thing set her off.

I lay there thinking about how much I hated her. Why had she found me? Why didn't I die? Or why didn't *she* take an overdose of yellow jackets and die?

My thoughts were interrupted as a doctor and a nurse entered my room. A smile filtered across the doctor's face when he saw I was awake.

"Well, young lady, you're looking better. I guess you can thank God for that."

I didn't respond. Mother didn't, either. Probably she still thought it would have been better if I had died. And yet she had found me and brought me here.

"Young lady," the doctor went on, "do you know why you're here?"

I looked at Mother, then back at the doctor. "Yes, I know. I passed out in the bathroom. The next thing I knew I was here."

"Partly right. You took an overdose of pills."

"Oh? Who told you that?"

"Your mother did."

I raised myself up on my elbows and glared at my mother. "Doctor, don't you believe a word that woman says. She'll tell anything to save her own skin. I've been very sick the last two weeks and have been in bed. All I know, doctor, is that I went to the bathroom, and the next thing I knew I was here. I don't know anything about any pills or whatever my old lady's talking about, but I do know she's a dirty liar. Don't believe her!"

Through the corner of my eye I could see Mother grit her teeth and clench her fist. I knew she wanted to strike out at me. But she couldn't—not with the doctor and nurse standing there!

No one talked. I rolled over to try to face the wall, but the needles in my arms made that extremely uncomfortable, so I had to roll back and lie flat on my back.

I couldn't imagine Mother not saying anything at all. I had probably humiliated her into silence. At least, that's what she would likely tell me later.

Finally the doctor said, "I'm sure, young lady, that you may want to change your story. But for now we'll just leave it at that. The most important thing to us is that you get well and get out of here as soon as possible."

When the doctor and nurse left, Mother shut the door behind them. What was she going to do?

Standing over me, she tried to talk quietly and

calmly, but her voice kept rising in anger. "Lori, whatever am I going to do with you? Why did you lie to that doctor? You know as well as I do that you popped those pills.

"Besides, I checked into how you got them. Peggy said she didn't know where they came from. Well, I knew you had been down to that drugstore, so I checked with the druggist. Sure enough, he said he was missing a bottle of those yellow pills. Don't you know they keep a running inventory of all their pills? They knew right away what was missing.

"Anyway, the druggist let your father pay for the pills. He said we had been doing business there for years, and he didn't want to cause us any embarrassment or any more problems.

"Problems? We've surely got them now. It's all over town, Lori, about your taking an overdose of pills."

I sneered, "Yes, Mom, your daughter's a junkie—a dirty, filthy, good-for-nothing junkie. She's taken an overdose. A real pill head. Oh, Mother, aren't you proud of me?"

I could hear her teeth gnashing together as she tried to control her anger. "Okay, Lori, you've done your thing and embarrassed me. I'm sure that's what you had in mind. But I'm going to tell you something, and I want you to get it straight. I've never told you this, but it's about time you learned a few things about your life."

Learn about my life? Whatever was she getting at? I had sensed for a long time now that something was bothering her. Maybe she was going to lay it all out.

"When your father and I got married," she began, "I didn't want children. To me kids are an annoyance and an interference. Well, in spite of everything, I got pregnant. My first thought was an abortion, but they were hard to get in those days. Besides, your father wasn't in favor of it, and he talked me out of it.

"Even so, Lori, I tried my best to miscarry. I'd go out in the woods and run as fast as I could when I was two months along with you. I jumped up and down. I'd even slam my fists into my stomach. But nothing happened.

"When you were born, Lori, I cursed. I mean, I cursed! I didn't even want to look at you."

So this was it. She had never wanted me. I knew she didn't really love me. Now I was beginning to understand why she acted so terribly toward me.

I wished she would stop. But I also was dying of curiosity to hear what else she had to say.

"You were an absolute nuisance," she went on, "and I even looked for ways I could give you up for adoption. Dirty diapers, screaming in the middle of the night to be fed, bawling, fussing—it was almost more than I could stand.

"I even tried to give you away, but no one would ever believe I was serious. And then your father kept blocking everything I tried to do, so I thought I'd better just learn to live with you."

Her eyes narrowed as she leaned over me. "Sure enough, you've turned out to be a beast, a real beast. I've had nothing but trouble with you ever since you were born. You know what I've gotten from you? Seventeen years of misery. I mean, absolute misery!"

The more she raged, the worse I felt. If only I had been born into another family where I had been wanted and loved!

She moved away from me and stared aimlessly out the window.

"To add to my misfortune," she continued, "about three years later Peggy was born. I came to accept her. She wasn't nearly as demanding as you. But something inside of me hated you. You completely fouled up my life and my plans."

She moved back to my bed.

"Lori, when you took that overdose and I looked at your still body on the bathroom floor, I thought my prayers were answered. I hoped you were dead!"

She paused to let that sink in.

"But Peggy had to rush into the bathroom about then. She's the one who picked you up and carried you to a neighbor's house. He rushed us here. So if you want to be alive, you can thank Peggy. If I had had my way, I'd have left you on that floor to rot. I wouldn't have moved one inch to save your life!"

That did it. Something within me exploded, and I screamed, "Get out of here right now! If I had a gun, I'd blow your face to smithereens!

"Mother!" I spat the word out in disgust. "You're not fit to even be called a mother. I want you out of my life forever. Go!"

"Shut your mouth, Lori. I'm not through yet."

Wildly I jerked the intravenous tubes from my arms. Mother's eyes popped wide open.

"Okay, if you want me dead," I yelled, "you can just stand there and watch me die. These things are keeping me alive, so just stand there and watch. Right in front of your miserable eyes my life will flow away. I'll give you your wish!"

She gnashed her teeth at me in anger. Then she turned and stalked out of the room.

Fluid from the bottle started dampening the sheets. I didn't care. But finally a nurse came in.

One look at me and she shrieked, "Young lady, what's happened? Don't you know we have that intravenous in your arms to keep you alive? Why didn't you call me?"

"I jerked them out on purpose," I answered without emotion.

"Jerked them out? Why? I mean, after all we've done

around here to save your life, why did you do
something like that? I'm going to have to go get the
doctor."

She hadn't even put the needles back into my arms.
But in a few minutes she was back, with the doctor and
two other men—big, tough ones, with belts in their
hands.

Before I could even protest or question, they had me
strapped down.

"Hey, Doc," I remonstrated, "you didn't have to do
that."

He just smiled. "We're taking a few precautions,
young lady. Our mission is to save people."

"Yes. Too bad everybody doesn't feel that way."

"What do you mean? Don't you want to live?"

"Well, Doc, even if I wanted to, that opinion isn't
shared by everybody. I mean, like my mother."

"What?" he demanded.

"Nothing. I guess nothing really matters."

He stared at me curiously but didn't pry any further.
The nurse jabbed the needles into my arms, and the
four of them walked out.

I tried to move, but the straps held me tightly, my
arms straight down alongside my thighs. All I could do
was stare at the stupid ceiling; I couldn't move a thing.
They really had me this time. No use struggling. . . .

I guess I dozed off—for how long, I don't know. But
when I slowly opened my eyes, I sensed someone
standing over my bed.

I blinked a few times and looked up into my father's
face.

"Oh, Lori, thank God you're alive!" he exclaimed.
"I've been so worried about you these past two days.
I've been here every minute I could spare, but you
didn't even know me!"

I managed a weak smile. Good old Dad. He always tried to be a good father to Peggy and me, even though he had to be gone a lot because of his work.

He was the one who always took us shopping and to school activities. He must have known how Mother felt about us and tried to make it up to us in some way.

I wished I had known years ago how Mother felt. Maybe I could have run away from home. Or maybe I could have had myself legally adopted. There's a lot said about children's rights these days. Maybe if I had gone to a judge and explained that my mother hated me and didn't want me, he'd have sent me to somebody else. But my father would never have accepted that. He always took care of us and loved us.

"The doctor told me what just happened in here," Dad said. "Lori, I need to know from you the real truth about the whole matter."

"Dad, I have absolutely nothing to say about it. Whatever you want to do, go ahead and do it. You can put me in prison; you can kill me; you can keep me strapped down like this for the rest of my life. Better yet, why don't you commit me to a mental institution and get me out of your life?"

"Lori, please, honey, don't talk that way. You know I love you very much, and I'll do everything I can to help you. You can count on me." Just like Dad—always trying to help.

"Lori, I've already talked to the police about what happened. Since this was the first time, they said they wouldn't press charges. But they warned that if something like this happened again, they'd have to take more drastic action. I've made restitution at the drugstore for those pills you stole. So when you get better, everything is going to be all right. But you've got to promise me that you won't try something like this again."

Dear, sweet, trusting Dad. Should I tell him how I hated Mother—and how she told me that she hated me? But would that really crush him?

"Lori, you must understand that your mother loves you very much. She was so stricken with grief these last two days; I've never seen her so concerned about you."

That did it! I couldn't take any lie like that!

"Dad," I blurted out, "that's a dirty, filthy lie! Mother was just in here and told me the whole story. She told me she didn't want me before I was born. She told me how she tried to miscarry and later how she tried to give me away. She said I was nothing but a nuisance, an intrusion in her life.

"I don't know if you know this, Dad, but she hates me. She stood right there where you're standing and told me that she wished I were dead!"

Tears of anger, frustration, and hurt gushed out. I wanted to bury my head in my hands, but I couldn't, strapped down as I was.

Dad didn't say a word. Was he really listening? Did he grasp what I had just said?

Between sobs I choked out some more. "Let me tell you something else, Dad. The other day Mother gave me a beating like I can't describe. She slapped me, pulled my hair, beat my head against the wall! You remember those puffed-up lips and bruises? Remember Mother said I had fallen down the basement stairs? I didn't fall down any stairs. Mother beat me! And then Peggy told me how Mother had beaten her on the legs so badly and then made her tell a lie about her bicycle being banged up in an accident. I mean that woman is sick, Dad, really sick!"

His features hadn't changed one iota during the whole time I was talking.

"Dad, are you listening to me?"

Ever so slowly he nodded his head. Then I noticed a big tear trickle down his cheek. Then another. And another. His body began to shake with sobs, and he fell on his knees and buried his head in the sheets of my bed.

Oh, how I wanted to reach out and comfort him, but the straps held me fast.

Then I felt hot tears start down my cheeks. My body began to quiver and shake as I sobbed along with him for I don't know how long.

Finally he pulled out his handkerchief and dabbed at his eyes. Then he clumsily tried to dry mine, gently smoothing back my hair and patting my cheeks.

He pushed himself to his feet, swallowed hard, and groped for the right words to say.

"You see, Lori, you're right. Your mother isn't at all well." He moved away and looked out the window, as if he couldn't look at me when he told this to me.

"There's a history of mental illness in your mother's family. Neither her mother nor her father were quite right. Both of her sisters and her brother are in mental hospitals.

"I know how she is, and I've tried my best to keep this from you because I knew what an embarrassment it would be to you if your friends found out that your aunts and uncle were in institutions. Nobody likes to think their relatives are crazy. I didn't want you and Peggy to worry about it.

"I'm very much aware of your mother's attitude. I knew she didn't want children. At the time I figured she was worrying about having children who weren't quite right mentally.

"After you were born, I had quite a struggle with her.

But I thought when she saw you were developing normally that everything would be okay. And things did seem to get better after Peggy was born. She accepted Peggy, but I sensed that she still hated you. That's why I tried my best to take you to the places where your mother wouldn't take you and do everything I could, but I knew it was a losing battle."

My throat tightened again, and tears flowed. Then it really was true. Mother did hate me, and she was sick.

Dad turned and saw me crying and came back and stood by the bed once again. "When I saw you the other day, I knew you hadn't fallen down the stairs. I figured that your mother had beaten you. But I didn't know what to do, so I didn't say anything."

"Dad, I think you'd better commit her to an institution; she's like a demon!"

"It's not that easy, Lori. She has been examined by psychiatrists. They say the mental institutions are filled with people who are much worse off. I know she probably needs help, but I just don't know what to do. I can't afford private treatment."

"Dad, you've got to do something quickly, or she'll kill me!"

"I know there's a problem, Lori. There must be some way out."

"Why don't you send her away to your family for a few weeks? Maybe they could take care of her."

Dad's face turned white. He started to say something, but words wouldn't come. Evidently I had hit on something. Curious, I decided to pursue it.

"Dad, why can't we send her to your relatives?"

He wheeled and walked back to the window again. He stood there silently for a long time, just staring out.

He never had said much about his family. Were they all mental cases, too?

Finally he came across the room, pulled up a chair, and sat next to my bed. "There's another side to the story, Lori. It's my family."

Well, Dad sure didn't seem like a mental case. He was just the opposite: loving, kind, warm.

"You see, Lori, my mother and father have both done time in prison. Your uncle George is now upstate in prison in Elmira. Aunt Vicky is doing time for bank robbery in Atlanta."

I just couldn't believe what I was hearing. Mother's side of the family was all crazy; Dad's side was criminal!

"I tried to keep this from you and Peggy. I knew it would be hard enough to explain mental problems on your mother's side. But to know you and Peggy had criminals on your father's side probably would have been more than you kids could handle."

"Dad," I said softly, "I've got to know. Were you ever in prison?"

He jumped up from the chair and returned to the window, ashamed to look me in the eye. I had my answer.

Finally he walked back over to the bed and sat on the edge of it. I knew what was coming.

"Do you remember when you were quite small and Mother told you I had to go out to the West Coast on a sales trip? Well, I didn't go out to the Coast. I had to serve time for robbery."

I still couldn't believe what I was hearing. It seemed like a nightmare. Maybe I was having a reaction from the yellow jackets. But Dad, standing there, seemed very real.

"Dad," I blurted out, "how could you ever do a thing like that?"

"I have no excuse, Lori. At the time money was a bit

tight, and sales were down. So I robbed a grocery store to help tide us over. But that was just an excuse. We were getting by even though things were a little tight."

He looked so embarrassed and guilty—like a kid who gets caught with his hand in the cookie jar. I knew I should say something to reassure and comfort him. But what?

The silence was so overwhelming that he finally mumbled, "I think I'd better be going." Without even kissing me good-bye, he turned and was gone.

There in the stillness of my room, wild thoughts raced through my head. Now I knew why my mother acted so terribly. She was crazy! And my father was an ex-con! It seemed as if no one on his side of the family had escaped being a criminal and no one on my mother's side had escaped being a mental case.

What did that make me? Criminally insane?

The more I thought about it, the more I concluded I would never have a chance in life. Someday the truth would be known. Could I stand that kind of pressure? Would I go to pieces, too?

I wondered how many of our neighbors already knew about our family. Surely they knew about Dad. They could read the papers. Did my friends know? How humiliating!

And what about when I got married and had children? What would I tell them? That their grandma and grandpa were crazy and criminal? Would my children turn out that way, too?

I could feel the rage flowing within me and I struggled against the straps that bound me. This horrible progression of craziness and criminality couldn't go on, generation after generation. I knew there was only one answer: suicide. Not just something to get even with Mother—the next time would be it!

FOUR

A week later I was released from the hospital. Naturally it was my father who picked me up. I would have flipped if Mother had come! She hadn't been to visit since that night when she told the truth about hating me.

Peggy was at the front door to greet me. She threw her arms around me and gave me a big hug and kiss. What would I ever do without her?

But there was no sign of Mother. She was probably in the bedroom pouting because I had come home. So what?

The three of us had coffee together and tossed around a lot of small talk, always carefully skirting the big issue. I kept wondering about Mother. It was strange that I couldn't even hear her stirring around somewhere in the house. When she sulked, she always wanted us to be aware that she was sulking.

Well, my curiosity finally got the best of me. "Where's Mom?" I blurted out.

Neither of them answered. Peggy avoided my gaze by staring at her coffee cup.

Dad looked as though he was trying to find the right words.

Don't tell me she couldn't take it anymore and split? Maybe she ran away from home! I should be so lucky!

"Okay, Dad, where's Mom?"

"She's gone for a few days, Lori."

I let out a sigh. "Well, isn't that just great!" I said sarcastically. "I hope she never comes back!"

Dad slammed his fist on the table, rattling the coffee cups until I thought for sure they would break.

"Don't ever say that again, Lori!" he exploded. "You know very well your mother isn't well. And if you must know the truth, she's in the hospital. She tried to kill herself!"

Peggy burst out crying, jumped up from the table, and ran for her bedroom. Dad sat there trembling.

Remorse hit me. I had said a very cruel thing, and I knew it was inexcusable. I knew what Mother's problem was. Couldn't I be a little more understanding? Dad probably still loved her—at least somewhat. After all, she was his wife. He was concerned about what happened to her. And two suicide attempts in his family within a week was probably just about as much as he could take.

"I'm sorry, Dad," I mumbled. "I didn't mean to say that." But Dad wasn't ready to let the matter rest.

"Lori, I think you and I need to get something straight. I'm trying to understand what you've been through and how it must feel to be rejected. But I'm also determined to do the best I can for your mother. If she ever needed help, it's right now. So if I can get your cooperation, I think we can help her get over this."

Now it was my turn to explode. "Say, that's just great. You're expecting me to come with my tail between my legs, aren't you—like an obedient, trustworthy, rever-

ent scout! Ha! As though Mother never laid a hand on
me. Well, let me tell you something, Dad. You must be
crazy, too! There's no way I want to help that woman.
No way. She hates my guts, and you know it! That's the
way I feel, and there's absolutely nothing I can do to
change it!"

"Now, now, just calm down, Lori. It really isn't all
that bad. There must be—"

I jumped up and interrupted, "Dad, I don't know if
you've ever been told you were hated. I don't know if
you've ever had someone tell you they wished you were
dead! Well, I've been told! I've been told that by
Mother in no uncertain terms. She doesn't want
anything to do with me. And I don't want anything to do
with her!"

Dad's restraint vanished again. "Lori, for crying out
loud, can't you understand what I'm trying to say?"

I yelled right back at him, "Can't you understand
what *I'm* trying to say?" I shook my finger in his face.
"That woman hates me and wants me dead!"

I gritted my teeth and screamed, "Okay, Dad, it's
either her or me! One of us will end up dead. Which
one, Dad?"

I guess I shouldn't have backed him into a corner that
way, but the words came out before I really had time to
think about them.

He just sat there, head bowed, hands encircling his
coffee cup.

"Okay, Dad," I yelled again, "who will it be—your
old lady or me?"

"Come on, Lori, please calm down. I know you are
upset. You just got home from the hospital. I don't want
to discuss anything like this. It's ridiculous!"

Ridiculous, was it? Well, this was going to be a

showdown. No way was I going to live under the same roof with that woman. One of us had to go.

I grabbed him by the shoulders and started shaking him. "Dad! Dad! Who is it going to be? Do you choose that beast of a woman or me?"

He shook himself free and stood up.

"Listen, Lori, I think you had better go to bed and calm down. I'm not used to having you talk to me this way."

"Who is it?" I screamed again. "Her or me?"

"Don't be ridiculous! I think you know. If you are going to force me into a corner and demand an answer, then I'll give you my answer. Naturally I choose your mother."

I let out a stream of curses. Something broke loose on the inside, and I just couldn't control myself. I lunged toward his throat like a wild animal. Then, slap, his hand cracked across my face, and I landed on the floor.

Bewilderment, frustration, anger—all those emotions rose within me as I looked up into his face.

"Lori, don't you ever try anything like that again!" With that anger in his eyes, he looked like a maniac. Maybe he was crazy, too.

I slowly rose, rubbing my face. Dad backed off.

Without a word I whirled down the hall to my bedroom and slammed the door. Obviously I wasn't wanted here.

I had a good cry, and then I started planning. Grabbing a suitcase out of the closet, I packed a few things, then stuffed the suitcase back into the closet again.

Nobody said much the rest of the day. Peggy had heard what had happened, and she just didn't know how to handle it. Well, I had a plan....

Late that night, when I was sure both Peggy and Dad were asleep, I grabbed my coat and suitcase, opened my bedroom window, and crawled out.

But my sense of freedom was short-lived. Where was I to go? What could I do?

I headed toward Angelo's Pizza—not because I was hungry, but because that's where some of the kids hung out. Maybe one of their families would put me up for the night. Tomorrow I could decide what I was going to do.

I was tired by the time I had walked the eight blocks to Angelo's. What dumb luck. Nobody was there but Angelo.

When he saw me, he began to laugh. "Hi, Lori. Haven't seen you for a while. Are you coming or going?"

I guess it did look stupid for me to be carrying a suitcase this close to home.

"Hey, Angelo, I'm heading on a long vacation and decided to stop for a pizza. I knew your pizza would get me there, no matter what."

He laughed again. "Come on now, kid. What's the matter?"

Good old Angelo. He was like a bartender. Everybody poured out his troubles to Angelo. He always seemed to understand.

"I'm running away from home," I sobbed, "and I don't know where to go!"

Coming out from behind the counter, he moved over next to me and put his arm around me. "Now, now, Lori," he said as he patted my shoulder, "things can't be all that bad. Tell me, what's the matter?"

Should I tell him? Would he understand? This really wasn't like a heartbreak because some boy wouldn't look at me!

"Oh, Angelo, nothing really," I answered as I dabbed away my tears. "Just a little misunderstanding."

"A little misunderstanding that makes you cry when I ask you what's wrong? A little misunderstanding that makes you pack your bags and leave home in the middle of the night? Come on, Lori, I've been around long enough to know it's more than that!"

"Well, it's just that my old man and old lady got kind of bad with me, so I thought I would cool it for a while."

Angelo gently pushed me toward a table. "Now, Lori, you sit down there, and I'll get us a couple of cups of coffee. This one's on me."

He was back in a minute, and I began to pour my heart out.

I couldn't bear to tell him that my mother hated me and had never wanted me or that she wished I were dead. But I did tell him about the beating and how my mom was crazy and my dad was a criminal—and how all this worried me.

He sat there quietly, nodding his head occasionally. He showed no surprise at the crazy-criminal bit. Did he already know?

We sat there in silence for a while, then he spoke.

"Lori, you must understand something about life. Mothers and fathers aren't perfect. They have problems just like kids have problems, only their problems are usually bigger. You know, it's mighty tough to raise kids these days.

"You worry that life has struck you a bad blow and that you were born into the wrong family. But let me tell you, you can take your hurts and turn them into something good if you try. You can rise above them instead of letting them destroy you. You've got what it takes, Lori. You're basically a good kid. I've always had confidence that you were going to make it."

Oh, that felt good. For the first time in years someone had confidence in me.

"One more thing," Angelo continued. "Let me give Martha a call. We've got an extra bedroom since Anthony went off to school. We're kind of lonely anyway, now that it's just the two of us. You can spend the night with us. Maybe things will look a little different in the morning."

That sounded so good, and what Angelo was saying made a lot of sense. Maybe I was hasty in leaving home the way I did.

Angelo had just started for the phone when the door of the pizza parlor opened and in walked an old friend, Joel Greenburg.

Good old Joel—everybody always called him "Cane Man." Whenever you saw Joel, you always saw his cane. He would strut around the block like a band leader. Or he would twirl it like a baton. He would jab you in the ribs with it or grab you or trip you. He would pound on garbage cans with it. But whenever you saw him, he had his cane. The two were inseparable.

As soon as he saw me, he ran over and playfully jabbed me in the ribs with that cane. "Hey, Lori baby! What are you doing with that suitcase? I mean, man, are you up to no good or something?"

"Just a little problem with my parents, that's all. Angelo's been giving me some fatherly advice."

Cane Man twirled his cane and laughed. "Hey, man, don't you know that parents are still living two hundred years ago? Why don't you get with it, Lori? Man, I beat it out of my house three years ago, and I'm never going back. My old man and old lady don't want me anyway." He caught the cane in midair and dropped it to his side.

"Don't want you?" I mimicked. "What's the matter?

Is your old lady a breadbasket case and your old man a criminal, too?"

"I wish it! I wish it!" Joel laughed excitedly. "Then I could lock my old lady up in a mental institution and see my old man in the pen for a few years. I could move back home and really live it up!"

Say, that might not be too bad an idea. I was ready for them to lock my old man up. My old lady was already gone. Peggy and I could have a blast!

"Hey, man, why don't you and I go out for a little walk? I'm sure we could get your head all straightened out. What do you say?"

Angelo was back from his phone call and sensed what was going on. "Now just a minute, Joel," he interrupted. "Lori and I were having a good talk. Don't you go interfering!"

"Angelo, Angelo, baby, calm down. You know me. I'm the best dude in the block. What I want to tell Lori she needs to hear. Understand?"

Angelo whispered, "Lori, that Cane Man is up to no good. You'd better stay away from him."

I knew I shouldn't go with him. But maybe if we talked for a little while it would help. His big smile made me wish I could be happy-go-lucky, the way he was. Maybe he had found the secret to life. I thought I'd at least try him out.

"Come on, Joel, what do you have that I don't have?"

"Baby, I've got the world by the tail. I mean, I know where it's at. Nothing bothers me. I'm on top of it all. Get it?"

What was he driving at? He looked as though maybe he was high on something.

Cane Man gently took my arm and pulled me up. He was easy to respond to. We headed toward the door.

"Lori, I'm telling you that Cane Man is no good!" Angelo yelled after us. "You mess with him, and you'll mess with your head. I mean, you're heading down a one-way street and there's no way to turn back. Don't go with that guy!"

Cane Man laughed. "Now, Angelo, I'm not going to touch Lori. You're a dirty old man who's always thinking about sex. As far as I'm concerned, Lori is just like a little sister to me. You can trust me, Angelo. I'm not going to touch her!"

As we walked through the door and down the street, Cane Man slipped his arm around me and squeezed. "Lori, you can trust me. I won't do anything your mommy and daddy would be ashamed of."

What was he getting at?

"Listen, Cane Man, I'm no pushover. You lay one hand on me, and I'll wrap that silly cane of yours around your neck and tie it in a knot! Yours eyes will bug out, and you won't mess with anybody anymore!"

He pushed back at arm's length and laughed. "Hey, you're a real little tiger, aren't you? Where have you been all my life? You sound as if you want me to challenge you!"

"Oh, come on, Cane Man. I've got bigger problems to worry about than something like that."

"Well, Lori, I've got the solution to your problems. You and I are going to get high together!"

"Get high? On what?"

"Well, I was on my way to buy some pot when I stopped in Angelo's. I want some of that stuff that is laced with PCP. I mean, that stuff will really give you a wallop. Like, I mean, it'll put you in orbit, and you'll never want to come down. Are you game?"

Marijuana laced with PCP—that was what everybody seemed to be using on the street. It really did something to you, they said. PCP was a drug they used to tranquilize horses, and it was strong stuff. I'd heard a lot about it but never had had the nerve to try it. But now I was ready for anything that might take my mind off my problems.

"Hey, why not?" I responded. "Have you got some?"

"That's just a little problem. I know where I can get some, but I'm flat busted."

"Don't look at me! I don't have a penny to my name!"

"Man, you're really nuts, aren't you? Running away from home without any money!"

He laughed at the ridiculousness of it.

"No matter," he said. "I know where I can get some money in a hurry, but I will need your help."

"Now, Cane Man, I'm not about to do anything that will get me in trouble with the cops."

"No way! Me neither. We just have to stay cool. As I said, you can trust me, man. All I'm going to do is borrow a little money for now."

I knew he was up to something, but, oh! how I wanted to get high. I had to get something to get me up.

We walked a few more blocks, neither of us saying much. Just before we got to a bar, Joel stopped, motioning me to stay there. He walked to the entrance, opened the door, and looked in. Then he quietly shut the door and walked back to me.

"Okay," he said, "let's wait around this corner. As soon as this guy comes out, I'll grab him with my cane and jerk on him."

"What do you mean, 'jerk on him'? Don't you know that a lot of guys in this neighborhood carry guns? If you monkey with them with that cane, they'll pull a gun and blow your brains out. No way am I going to get messed up in something like that!"

"Come on, man, you don't know how this cane works. Here, let me show you."

Before I could blink my eyes Cane Man had the cane around my neck. I tried to flip it away, but he just pulled harder. All of a sudden I felt as if I were going around in circles, and the pain was almost unbearable. The cane was choking me, and I was pulling with all my might to get away. Then just as suddenly he released me.

I jerked away and screamed, "You idiot! You almost killed me with that thing!"

He just smiled. "That's what I'm talking about, man. And I want you to notice something. When that cane went around your pretty little neck, what did you do?"

"What do you mean, what did I do? I was trying to get it loose, you dummy!"

"That's what I'm talking about, man! Now tell me, where were your hands?"

I thought for a moment. "Why, my hands were on that cane trying to get it away from my neck because you were choking me to death! Where did you expect them to be?"

"Man, you catch on quickly. Now tell me, if you had a gun in your pocket, do you think you would be reaching for a gun when you were choking to death? No way, baby! This cane is the most effective weapon in the neighborhood! Nobody will pull a gun on me when I'm pulling on his neck!"

He had a point.

"Now, man, this is what we'll do. It won't be long before one of those drunken bums stumbles out of that bar. What we'll do is so simple you'll want to be doing it twenty-four hours a day! As soon as he turns this corner, I'll get him with this cane and jerk him. I'll jerk him over this garbage can, and he'll flip over. As soon as he flips, you grab his wallet and run. I'll be right behind you."

It did sound simple. But as we stood there for a couple of moments in the darkness, my heart pounded.

Then the tavern music got louder, and we knew the door had opened. We pushed back against the wall to wait. I could hear the man shuffling along. My hands quivered in fright.

I could see his shadow. Then his form. Cane Man whipped out his cane and had him around the neck before the poor guy knew what was happening. Cane Man jerked, and the guy sailed over the garbage can. Cane Man had done that before!

Now for my part. I reached for his hip pocket. What? No pockets? Oh, no! I suddenly realized it was an old lady!

She started to scream. "Hit her in the mouth!" Cane Man yelled. "Hit her in the mouth, you dummy!"

I clenched my fist and looked at the old woman. She just stared at me, terrified.

Then she started to scream again. I rammed my hand over her mouth to stifle her.

"No! No!" Cane Man yelled again. "Hit her in the mouth! Hit her in the mouth!"

I couldn't. "I just can't hit an old lady."

"Do as I tell you! If she doesn't stop screaming, the cops'll be here in a second!"

"I can't hit her!"

"Hit her!"

"I can't!"

"Hit her, man. It's my grandmother. I can't hit my own grandmother!"

That was it. I clenched my fist and came down as hard as I could. Her lips quivered, and her eyeballs rolled back. She was losing consciousness.

"Hit her again!"

Just as the woman started to scream, my fist came down hard. Blood splattered across her face, and she slumped to the ground.

Cane Man grabbed her purse, and then he grabbed me. "We have to get out of here, quick!"

We tore down the block, turned the corner, and ran three more blocks and up into an alley. Halfway up the alley we stopped, both of us completely out of breath.

We leaned up against the building, and Cane Man rifled through the old lady's purse for her wallet. He grabbed some bills, stuffed them in his pocket, and threw the purse in a garbage can.

"Come on!" he ordered. "We can't stay here!"

We took off again, but not quite so fast this time.

About three blocks away I called out, "Cane Man, I can't go on." I was scared and out of breath. I still wasn't too strong from that hospital ordeal. So we stood in some shadows next to an old garage.

"Cane Man," I panted, "how in the world could you mug your own grandma?"

He laughed. "Oh, come on, dummy. That wasn't my grandmother. Do you think I would have said something like that if that was my grandmother? She would have known who it was and reported it to the police! Man, you'll have to get with it.

"The problem is, they'd put me away for many years for hitting an old lady. That's one thing a man can't do—hit an old lady. But a woman hitting an old lady doesn't make much difference to a judge. So if we ever get busted, the rap will go easier on you than it would have on me."

Get busted? Oh, no! Now I had really done it—and something else. I couldn't get that woman's face out of my mind. Poor thing—those quivering lips; those eyeballs sinking; that terrified, pleading look; the blood all over her face.

I just knew the pain was excruciating. And flipping her over that garbage can—she had landed with quite a thud. Maybe we had even broken her shoulder!

Cane Man grabbed my arm, and we headed down the street.

"Where are we going?" I asked.

"We'll take a subway to Forty-second Street. Man, you can buy all kinds of drugs there. You can get cocaine, heroin, pot, PCP, HCP, and the scientists only know what else. It's as open as it can be."

It wasn't long until we were at Eighth Avenue on Forty-second Street. Even at three o'clock in the morning there were still a lot of people around.

It didn't take Cane Man long to cop his pot. One guy even came up to him and asked him if he wanted to buy some! I hoped it wasn't a rip-off. I had heard kids tell how sometimes they bought some stuff and later on found out it was absolutely nothing! Pot laced with horse manure. Pills with flour in them. Even heroin that contains only milk sugar.

Cane Man and I headed for an alley and lit up. I took a long drag and got it settled to my lungs.

The feeling came on slowly but kept getting more intense. A couple more drags, and I felt myself going into orbit....

I don't know how long I was up there, but when I came down, I looked around. I was in a room. Over on the floor leaning up against the wall was Cane Man—fast asleep.

Hey, what was I doing in bed? And with just my underclothes on? What had happened? What day was it? How did I get from Forty-second Street to here? And where was I?

My head hurt, and I felt dizzy. I climbed out of bed to look for my clothes. Finally I found the bathroom. There they were, crumpled on the floor.

I had this horrible thought about what could have happened in the last few hours—or days. Had Cane Man touched me? Was I pregnant? And where was I?

I shook my blouse and jeans out and slipped them on. Then I wandered around some more until I found my shoes. I went over and shook Cane Man awake.

"Cane Man, where are we?"

He squinted his eyes, and then he laughed. "Hey, baby, we're home! I mean, this is my pad. Don't worry about a thing!"

I went over and sat on the edge of the bed. Dirt and filth were everywhere. I buried my head in my hands. If this was being happy-go-lucky, I didn't want any part of it.

Just then someone knocked on the apartment door. Cane Man motioned for me to answer it.

There stood two well-dressed men. One of them flashed a badge. "We're from the police department. Can we talk to you for a minute?"

I started to slam the door, but he already had his foot in it. He easily pushed his way in.

Oh, no! How could they possibly have tailed us here so quickly? I didn't even have time to find out where I was. But where was I going now—to jail?

FIVE

The words *police department* brought Cane Man to his feet. "Hey, man, what's going on here? We didn't do anything!"

"No, we didn't do anything," I echoed. "We were just here minding our own business!"

"Now calm down, you two. We just want to ask you a few questions, that's all. I didn't say you were up to anything, did I?"

"No, but you sound as though you're ready for a bust," Cane Man replied.

What kind of trouble is Cane Man in? I wondered. They wouldn't suspect him for that mugging yet. Were they looking for him on some other rap?

"Okay, you two, what were you doing on Tuesday night?"

He had me there. When was Tuesday? I really had no idea. How long ago had I gotten high on that PCP?

"Excuse me, officer; I don't have my calendar with me. How many days ago was that?"

"Well, this is Friday, so that was three nights ago. Where were you?"

Friday already? Wow!

"Well, I was right here last Tuesday," Cane Man responded. "You see, I'm a college man, and I was right here studying for a test. I mean, I was studying hard. I'm a junior at Queens College."

"And you, young lady?"

I mumbled a little and then blurted out, "I'm a freshman at Queens. Cane Man and I were studying together, weren't we, Cane Man?"

No response.

"Young lady, what is your name?"

I didn't know whether to lie or not. I knew that once they caught me in a lie, I'd be pretty well judged guilty. So I decided I'd better tell them my right name.

"I'm Lori Hutton."

One of the officers pulled out a pad and pen. "And where do you live?"

"I stay here with Cane Man."

"What do you mean, 'Cane Man'? You keep talking about Cane Man. Who in the world is he?"

Cane Man smiled. "That's me, officer. I'm Cane Man, the best dude in town."

"Okay, sonny, what's your real name?"

"Like I told you, it's Cane Man. The first name is Cane, and the second name is Man."

I knew I shouldn't, but I couldn't help laughing. Cane Man could make fools out of these cops!

"Okay, don't get smart with me. I might as well tell you right out that we're looking for someone who was involved in the mugging of an old lady. Now let's get a few facts straight, and don't smart off this time. Now, what is your real name?"

Cane Man glanced at me, and then he got serious. "Okay, officer. I don't know anything about any mugging or any old lady. My name is Joel Greenburg."

"Okay, Lori Hutton. Give me your address."

"My address is right here. I told you that before."

"Okay then, what is your address right here?"

He had me. I had no idea where I was. But I had to think of something quickly.

"I mean, you see, my address has been here for just a few days, and I don't have it memorized. Cane Man, tell the officers what the address is here."

"Ten forty-six One hundred fifty-fourth Street."

"Okay then, lady, tell me some of your teachers at Queens College. I'm going to night school. Maybe I'll recognize some of them."

What rotten luck! Could I give a false name?

All of a sudden I blurted out, "Louise Turner."

"Louise Turner? There's no Louise Turner I know of teaching at Queens. Is she new there?"

"Yes, she just started a couple of weeks ago. Fantastic teacher! I've got her for psychology. You mean you haven't heard of her?"

"Sorry, I've never heard of her. Let's try another."

I thought for a moment. Then another name flashed through my mind. "Maureen O'Daly."

"Maureen O'Daly? Now come on, lady. There's no Maureen O'Daly teaching at Queens College."

Was this officer bluffing? There were hundreds of teachers at Queens College. He couldn't possibly know them all.

Then he grabbed my arm. "Listen, kid, there's no sense in lying to us. If you don't start telling the truth, we're going to haul you in. So listen very carefully. You stop lying and start giving us some straight answers. Do you understand?"

My bravado faded, and I answered meekly, "Yes, sir."

"Okay, let's try again. What is your address—and I

mean your real address, not this address, Cane Man's address, or the address of Queens College. I want to know where you live." He pointed his finger at my face.

Without hesitating I blurted out, "Fourteen fifty-six One hundred forty-ninth Street, Queens."

Satisfied that he was getting the truth, he wrote it down.

"Okay, now I'll tell you what this whole deal is all about. We're looking for a teenager. On Tuesday at about two o'clock in the morning an old lady was mugged. Her assailant slammed her in the face, and her shoulder was broken in the scuffle. The old lady gave us a good description of the woman who hit her. I must tell you, Miss Hutton, that you fit it perfectly!"

My heart popped into my throat and started pounding wildly. How could they possibly know it was me? And how did they find me so quickly here in Cane Man's apartment?

Cane Man wasn't saying a word, so I decided to play it cool. This officer had to be bluffing.

"Officer, I don't have the slightest idea what you're talking about. You have Cane Man's word that I was here with him last Tuesday night."

"Well," the officer responded, "Cane Man, if that's what you call him, isn't a suspect in this case. The old lady said there were two people, but the only person she saw was a girl of your description.

"We've been checking that neighborhood for clues. The owner of a pizza parlor told us he had seen Cane Man in the area that night and gave us his description."

That dirty Angelo!

"The woman says the only thing she remembers when she came out of the bar was being jerked over a garbage can and then there was a girl of your description hitting her in the face. That's all she remembered before she lost consciousness. It was a good thing somebody found her when they did, or you might be facing a murder rap!"

I walked over and put my arms around Cane Man's waist. "Listen, officer, there's no way you can pin that on me. As I told you, I was right here on Tuesday night, wasn't I, Cane Man?"

No response. *Hey, wait a minute! He got me into this!* Surely he would speak up for me.

He roughly shoved me away.

"Officer," he said in a confidential tone, "I really must level with you...."

Don't tell me he was going to confess? That dumb nut!

"You see, officer, the truth is that I was here studying on Tuesday night, but I don't want anybody implicating me in any mugging, you see. This Lori wasn't in my apartment studying. She doesn't go to Queens College. I met her before, and, well, she ended up here at about four o'clock in the morning high as a kite. I just couldn't turn her away. And that's the truth!"

That dirty, rotten, filthy—he'd do anything to save his own skin!

Once again something snapped inside me, and the next thing I knew I had hauled off and slugged Cane Man in the face. He raised his fist to return the blow, but just then the two officers separated us and pushed me up against the wall. Before I knew what was happening, they flipped out their handcuffs and pinned my hands behind my back.

"Kill the witch! Kill the witch!" Cane Man screamed. "I mean that dirty, filthy, rotten liar! You try to help somebody, and what do you get for it? Get her out of my sight before I tear her limb from limb! I mean, get her out of here now!"

"Officer, so help me, I'm not taking this rap alone! Now let me tell you the truth!" I yelled.

Here I was, pinned against the wall, unable to defend myself, and Cane Man came rushing at me, his cane raised menacingly. But the other officer put his foot behind Cane Man and pushed him back. Cane Man sprawled unceremoniously on the floor. Before he had a chance to do anything, that officer pounced on his back and flipped handcuffs on him, too.

I looked at him with utter disdain as he lay there kicking and screaming. I yelled, "Okay, I'll tell you the truth. I've got evidence to back up what I'm saying."

"Don't believe her," Cane Man screamed. "She's no good. You saw what she did to me!"

"Officer," I blurted out, "we did rob an old lady Tuesday night. But I didn't do it myself. It was Cane Man's idea. I just went along with it. In fact, I didn't want to hit the old lady. I'm not that kind of a girl. But he screamed at me that I had to hit her. He lied to me and said it was his grandmother and that he couldn't hit her. Can you imagine anybody letting someone hit his grandmother? Officer, he's the one who's no good. He's the one who's going to carry this rap—not me!"

Cane Man struggled to his feet and started toward me, letting out oaths that turned the air blue.

One of the officers stepped between us. "Okay, you two, I don't know who's lying and who's telling the truth, but we're going to find out. You're both under arrest!"

I couldn't believe this was really happening to me. I'd never been arrested before.

One officer grabbed my arm and pushed me out the door. Cane Man was kicking and cursing, so the officer grabbed him around the neck. He squeezed tightly, and Cane Man got the message.

Down at the station I was terribly embarrassed as they questioned us some more. Then I was hustled to a back room for a mug shot and fingerprinting.

Finally a matron led me to a cell. As the door clanged shut behind me, I slowly moved to a hard, wooden bench.

I was stunned. I couldn't believe where I was—all alone in this cold, dark, damp, smelly cell. What a dirty, lousy, filthy deal! What a fool I was for listening to Cane Man!

Later the matron returned to check on me. I asked her what would happen next. She explained that in the morning I would be taken to court, arraigned, and then, unless I made bail, I would be transferred to the women's prison at Rikers Island to wait for trial.

Trial! The very word mocked me. "What do you mean, trial?" I screamed. "You are treating me just like a criminal without any rights!"

She laughed. "Treating you like a criminal without rights, are we? How else should we treat you—like a princess?"

"Listen, lady, I want out of this jail, and I want out now. Do you understand?"

"Yes, I understand. We don't get many who really want to stay here!" She looked at me mockingly. "You were read your rights when they brought you in here. If you want to make a telephone call, we'll let you do that. Do you want to call somebody?"

I sure did. But who? Who would care enough to help me? Dad? Well, he'd probably be worried about me. He was my only hope. Now, if the bail weren't too high. . . .

At my arraignment the next morning bail was set at one thousand dollars. I was allowed to use the phone, and I called my dad.

Peggy answered. I could hear her screaming to someone, "It's Lori! It's Lori!"

In a moment I heard my father on the other end of the line. "Lori, is that you?"

"Yes, Dad, it's me."

"What happened? Where have you been? Angelo brought your suitcase over and told me you had gone with that Cane Man. Are you all right?"

"Yes, Dad, I'm fine. But I got into a little trouble. I got pulled in on a charge of mugging an old lady, and I'm down here in jail. Could you come down and bail me out?"

Silence.

"Dad, please?"

"Lori, tell me the truth. Did you really mug that woman?" I knew I'd better level with him. He knew what it was to be accused of a crime. He'd understand.

"Yes, Dad. But I'm really sorry, and I—"

Click!

I banged on the receiver and screamed, "Don't do that! Please don't do that! Please! Please! You can't do this to me!"

The matron walked over. "What happened?"

"My old man just hung up on me!"

"Too bad."

Too bad? That was easy for her to say. She wasn't the one who was going to rot in that stinking cell! Desperately my mind searched for some way out.

"Maybe he didn't hang up! Maybe we got disconnected! Oh, matron, do you think something went wrong?"

"Well, I don't know," she sympathized. "Once in a great while something goes wrong with the telephone— or maybe your dad got nervous and accidentally cut you off."

"That's it! That's it! I know my dad would never hang up on me. I'm sure we got cut off. Can I make another call? Please?"

"I'm sorry, the rules are one call."

I started jumping up and down and screaming, "Don't you know if my dad doesn't come down here and bail me out, I'll probably rot in some cell? Please, please let me make one more call. I'm begging you on my knees. I don't have any money, but my father will pay you back when he comes for me. Please! Please!"

People were staring. Any other time I would have felt like a fool. But desperation does strange things to a person.

The matron stared coldly at me. "Regulations say one phone call, and you've had yours."

I buried my head in my knees and sobbed and sobbed. The end of the world had come for me.

Then I felt her hand on my shoulder. "Okay, you don't need to take it so hard. I know this is your first time. There's nothing in the regulations about *my* making a phone call. I'll see if you got disconnected."

I jumped to my feet and told her the number. It seemed as though it took her ages to dial it.

I heard her say, "This is Florence Olsen at the Fifty-sixth Precinct. We have a suspect under arrest here by the name of Lori Hutton. She claims she was talking to her father and got cut off. Is this Mr. Hutton?"

I waited. She nodded her head up and down several times. "I see. I see. Yes, I understand. Well, thanks anyway. I just wanted to be sure."

Before I knew what was happening, the matron hung up the receiver.

"What's the matter with you?" I yelled. "Why didn't you let me talk to my father?"

"You were right the first time, Lori. Your father said

he didn't want anything else to do with you. As far as he was concerned, you could rot in jail."

I stood there in total disbelief. Not my father, too! He wouldn't treat me this way! He had always been there when I needed him before!

"Okay, lady, back to your cell."

I can't explain the feeling of total aloneness and hopelessness I felt when the cell door clanged shut behind me. I didn't even sit on the hard bench. I just stood there in the middle of that cell, staring blankly into space. As sure as anything I would face a prison term—and no one cared. My mother obviously didn't care what happened to me. Cane Man—that dirty rat—wouldn't lift a finger for me. And now, my father didn't care. Nobody cared!

The next morning they transferred me to the prison on Rikers Island. For the first time I was placed in a cell block with a bunch of other girls—foulmouthed and abusive ones. A couple of them were lesbians and tried to approach me. I got really angry with them, and they backed off.

Sleep was almost impossible that night. The cot was unbelievably lumpy. The snoring of some of the girls just about drove me crazy. There was no way prison life would be for me. I had to find a way out—even if I had to kill myself.

Kill myself! Yes, that was it! Nobody cared what happened to me, anyway. Who would even miss me? Suicide was the only way out of this mess.

At about two o'clock in the morning, when I guessed everyone was asleep, I crawled out of my bunk and started to look for something I could slash my wrists with. Surely one of these girls had a mirror. I walked between the rows of beds, looking, searching. Nothing.

Discouraged, I walked back and sat on the edge of

my bed. As I did, my hand slid underneath and touched the sharp edge of a bolt. *It's worth a try!* I thought.

I pushed my wrist lightly across it. Nothing happened. Harder. The pain was excruciating as I felt the sharp edge of the bolt cut my skin. But it just scratched the surface, and only a few drops of blood came.

I got down on my knees and slid under the bed. Vigorously I rubbed my wrist back and forth against the bolt. Now it was really bleeding.

I took the other wrist and did the same thing. The gash wasn't very deep, but the blood kept coming. Harder and harder I pushed. Deeper and deeper. Now I was getting somewhere, but I almost passed out from the pain. I couldn't risk being found on the floor.

Blood was coming from my wrists profusely now. With great effort I pulled myself back into bed. I held my wrists over the edge and let the blood splatter on the floor.

I wondered what it would be like to die. What happened to a person after death? Was there another life? Well, if there was, at least I'd be out of jail!

Just then I saw a flashlight playing along the rows of sleeping girls. I heard footsteps approaching. The matron!

I jerked both arms under the covers and lay there perfectly still with my eyes closed. The bright light hit my face, and I heard her exclaim, "What is going on here?"

I tried to act sleepy. I slurred my words and said, "What's going on where? Can't a body get any sleep around this place?"

"What's this blood all over the floor?"

"Blood? What blood?"

I rolled over and looked down. Just then she jerked

back the covers and saw blood coming from my wrists.
Without a word she wheeled away and was gone.

Was she just going to let me die?

In minutes she came rushing back with two men.
They grabbed me and half-carried me into a small
infirmary and strapped me down. One of them cleaned
the wounds and bandaged them.

No one said a word. I guess they were used to this
kind of thing happening. Other girls must have faced
the same desperation I did.

When they had finished, the matron came back.
"Okay, lady, it'll have to be an isolation cell for you,"
she said matter-of-factly. "We don't take kindly to
people trying to commit suicide in our prison. It makes
us look bad."

That made me furious. They didn't care whether I
lived or died—so long as they didn't look bad!

The isolation cell had absolutely nothing in it—just
four bare walls and a bare floor. No bed. No bench.
Nothing!

"What am I supposed to sleep on?"

"Try the floor, honey. You got yourself into this
pickle."

I was still seething with anger over their attitude and
over botching that suicide attempt. If I got another
chance, I wouldn't botch it. There had to be some way
out. But there was no way in this cell. They had seen to
that.

I glanced at the top of the bars. *Hey! If I could find
something to hang myself from there, I would make it.*

Obviously they didn't leave a length of rope in an
isolation cell. What could I use to hang myself with?

Then it hit me. I could do it with my blouse and my
bra.

I jerked my blouse off and twisted it. Then I

unsnapped my bra and tied the two together. I tied one end to the bar as high up as I could. Then I tied the other end around my neck.

I cinched the knot tight. Of course, there wasn't anything I could kick out from under my feet, so I simply let myself slump to the floor.

As I did that, the knot tightened around my neck. I gasped for air, but none came. Then I blacked out.

SIX

I can't breathe! I can't breathe!

Something was over my mouth, choking me. I rolled my head back and forth, trying to get away from whatever it was that held me.

What are those long, spiderlike things running to my mouth? If this is hell, it certainly is weird!

Gradually my mind cleared, and I could see the matron and those two fellows. The thing over my mouth? It had to be an oxygen mask.

"Breathe deeply!" the matron ordered.

I breathed deeply.

"More!" she ordered again. "Just stay cool, and everything is going to be okay."

So I hadn't died. Evidently someone had found me and brought me to this room.

Satisfied that I was going to make it, they pulled away the oxygen mask.

"What happened?" I asked.

"What happened?" one of the guys echoed incredulously. "Now don't just lie there and try to act dumb. You tried to hang yourself!"

"I know that, you stupid jerk. I mean how did I get here?"

"Baby, you were just really lucky," the matron replied. "Regulations require us to check isolation regularly. When I went by your cell, you were sprawled on the floor, unconscious. We dragged you in here and gave you a shot of oxygen. You can thank God you're still alive. If I had been a few minutes later, I'm afraid it would have been too late!"

I just stared at the ceiling. Why did she have to come when she did? And why should I thank God for being alive? How could a person thank God when she had been cut off from everyone? From her mother, from her father, from her friends. I had gotten busted, and nobody cared a hoot whether I lived or died. Oh, yes, the matron cared. It would look bad for her if I committed suicide! Thank God? I'll bet even God didn't care what happened to me—if there was a God.

"Okay," I said, "I feel better now. What's next?"

"Well, it's back to isolation for you," the matron sneered. "You didn't expect us to let you go free now, did you?"

I raised my head off the table and suddenly realized I was stark naked! I grabbed for the sheets. Nothing! I threw my arms around to cover myself as best I could.

Oh, that made me mad. "Okay, you guys. This is not a nudist colony. You stop staring, or I'll have you both arrested!"

They laughed at that idea.

"It's not funny! Now give me back my clothes!"

Both of them just stood there. The matron turned and walked away. Oh, no! Was she going to leave me here at their mercy?

I bolted for the door, but they were too fast. Both of them grabbed me. One of them clamped his hand over my mouth. "Listen, you little twerp. You just keep your mouth shut. Do you hear?"

I knew what was going to happen next. Rape! I'd heard of prisoners raping other prisoners and even of guards raping prisoners. So help me, if I ever got out of this place, I was going straight to the district attorney. These two jerks would pay for this crime!

"Okay, lady, just calm down. You won't get hurt if you cooperate."

Cooperate, my foot! I kicked and screamed and kicked some more.

Then I felt that big hand clamped over my mouth once more. "Listen, lady, will you stop that? We've got to take you back to isolation. I'm sorry about your clothes. But since you used them to try to hang yourself, we have no recourse but to take you back just the way you are—no clothes at all."

He looked right into my eyes. Then he slowly 'ropped his hand from my mouth. "I know what you're thinking, young lady, and I'm sorry if we gave that impression. But it just isn't so. I have a lovely wife and three girls at home, and what you're thinking isn't going to happen. Understand?"

I didn't say a word.

He opened the door, and we walked down the hall. Other employees passed us, but they didn't seem to notice. I felt so humiliated. To walk naked down that hall was one of the most devastating experiences I have ever had. I felt exposed to the whole world!

When we got back to the isolation cell, one of the guards told me, "We'll work a little deal with you. We're going to leave you without any clothes for the next four hours. If you behave yourself and don't cause any commotion, then we'll start giving your clothes back to you one piece at a time. Now we're going to be checking on you. If you cause any commotion, no clothes. Understand?"

I nodded. I wasn't about to do anything to ruin the chances of getting my clothes back.

They stepped out and locked the door.

Like a whipped puppy I went over into a corner of that bare cell and sat down. Oh, the floor was cold, and I had nothing to keep me warm.

Staring into space blankly, I began to think of all the trouble I had caused various people. Two suicide attempts in one night. I guess it was a stupid thing to do. There must be a better way out of this jail.

It seemed like an eternity that I waited for my clothes. But about four hours later the cell door opened. The guard held out my panties.

I snatched them from his hand. As I started to slip them on, he looked the other way.

"Thanks, sir."

"I'm very sorry it's got to be this way, but somehow we have to teach you a lesson. Any time there's a suicide in this place, it looks bad on our record, and the media is always bugging to have an investigation.

"We really should have handcuffed you, but I think maybe you've learned your lesson. There's something about you that seems different from the other girls who come here. If you try hard, little girl, you can make it."

He stepped outside and locked the door. In another thirty minutes or so he returned with my bra. Once again he turned around as I put it on.

"Thanks again, sir."

He turned around and smiled. Then from under his coat he pulled out a dress. "Here, put this on quickly, and don't start to thank anybody that you got the dress and the bra at the same time. I think that dress will fit you—and I think you've gone through enough!"

I grabbed the dress and pulled it over my head. As I did, he turned around and was facing the wall again.

I just couldn't get over that.

"Sir," I said, "what you're doing is almost stupid. You saw me stark naked when you hauled me in here. Yet when you gave me my clothes, you turned around and didn't look. What gives?"

He smiled. "I've been a guard here for almost fifteen years now. I've talked to many, many girls like you. And I've learned a lot of things I've been able to take home to my own three daughters. One of the things I've learned is that teenagers and older girls hardly ever recover if their father sees them naked. They are so ashamed of that. I've determined I never would let that happen to my daughters.

"Now I know it seems strange, but every once in a while, in the line of duty, we have to take a girl's clothes off because she tries to hang herself. Your attempt isn't all that unusual. Lots of girls become overwhelmed with their problems, and some of them think suicide is the way out. Well, anyway, I guess I just want to show these girls that I have some respect for them; so when they're dressing, I'm not going to look. Maybe my respect will let them know that there's at least one person in this prison who cares. I do care what happens to you, young lady."

"Oh, come on. You don't even know me. I'll bet you don't even know my name or why I'm here."

"That's partly true. But I do know your name, Lori, and I do know you're here because you're in trouble—probably deep trouble. Frankly, this is no place for a girl to be. We've got women in here who are murderers, or are prostitutes, or are perverted. A whole bunch of them are lesbians. This is no place for a clean-looking girl like you."

He paused and then continued. "I did take a look at

your record and found out you didn't have mental illness and that you were charged with mugging. But you just don't seem the type to spend the rest of your life in prison."

I could certainly agree with that. I had never considered myself prison material.

"And furthermore, young lady, when you do get out of here, give life a chance. Go straight."

He turned and walked out, shutting the door. Wait a minute! I didn't hear it lock! Maybe this was my break!

I stood there a few moments while his footsteps moved away. Then I sneaked over to the door and pushed against it ever so slightly. It wasn't locked! Wow!

I heard footsteps down the hall and quietly pulled the door shut.

Now why did he fail to lock that door? Did he want me to escape? He said I didn't belong in a place like this. Or did he just forget?

I needed time to think, so I went over and sat on the floor again. It felt better to have clothes on. It's amazing how secure you get when you aren't stark naked!

I still didn't have a plan, but I knew I couldn't wait very long. Someone would be by here again soon to check on me.

I got up and inched toward the door. I pushed it lightly. It really was unlocked! I peered down the hall. No one was in sight. Maybe I could escape. But deep inside I knew that one unlocked door wouldn't get me out of this prison. Yet, it was a start.

Footsteps again. I pulled the door shut and went back over and sat down. This time the footsteps kept coming and finally stopped in front of my cell.

"Well, I see you're still with us," the matron said matter-of-factly.

"What do you mean, still here? Did you expect me to

run out of here and climb over the wall?"

"Hardly!" Then she laughed. "But with you, I just never know. Of course, if you did get out of your cell, you'd have to go through some more locked doors. And if you did escape out of the compound, you would have to climb a fence. There are guards all around that—with guns. And after you climbed the fence, you'd have to swim for it. You see, it would be a long road if you tried to get out. As far as I know, no woman has ever escaped from Rikers Island!"

"Well, I'm not going anyplace."

"That's good. Now I think we can take you out of isolation."

"Say, matron, I noticed when you walked into my cell, the door wasn't locked. How come?"

"Oh, you noticed, did you? Well, that was just a little test. When Weaver left you the last time, he purposely left your cell unlocked. He was just down the hall waiting to see what you would do. If you had come running out of your cell, we would have had to keep you in isolation for a little longer. But you passed the test. So you can go back with the other girls."

I drew a deep sigh. I sure was glad I hadn't tried to escape. I would have run right into Weaver's arms and then back into this cell—for goodness knows how long. I think I would have lost my mind if I had had to stay in isolation very long.

The matron led me back to the room where I had been the night before—the large room with the little cubicles for each girl. I went over and sat on the edge of my bed. Out of curiosity I felt for the sharp bolt. Gone!

I settled into the dreary routine of prison life for a few weeks. My wrists started to heal, but the scars looked horrible. What a reminder of my foolishness. Would they ever go away?

My every waking thought was to find some way out of this mess. Maybe when my trial came up I could plead insanity. It did run in the family.

When I awoke one morning, I found they had brought in a new girl during the night. I guess she had heard about me from one of the other girls, for she singled me out for special attention.

"Why did you try to knock yourself off?" she asked.

I started to tell her it was none of her business, but she seemed so friendly and outgoing that instinctively I knew I could trust her.

"I really don't know why," I answered. "It was kind of a stupid thing, I guess."

She flipped her long, brown hair back. My, she was beautiful! But she popped her gum incessantly.

"Hey, sweetheart, you'd better believe that was a stupid thing to do. You get nowhere if you go that route. Baby, that's hell, and I mean real hell. There's a much better life for you than that."

How dare she talk about a better life? She was in prison—just like me!

"What are you doing time for?" she asked. "For pros?"

"For what?"

"For pros. Pros. Hey little girl, don't you know what that means?"

"No, I've never heard of it."

"Hey, you'd better get wise—I mean real wise. *Pros* means prostitution. You're a cute little number, too cute to rob banks. So you must be in here for prostitution. Right?"

"Wrong! I wouldn't want to get into that. I mean those girls are filthy and dirty and don't know what they're doing and are full of social disease."

"Hey, sweetheart, why do you think I'm here?"

Uh-oh! I goofed on that one. She must be charged with prostitution. But she was very friendly and very attractive, and certainly no junkie—not at all the way I had expected a prostitute to be.

"The name's Michelle. Michelle Timmins."

"Hi, Michelle. I'm Lori Hutton."

"Okay, Lori Hutton, what are you doing here?"

"Oh, I did a stupid thing. I went out with this guy. To get money for drugs, we mugged an old lady. When the cops closed in, the guy ratted on me—said I was the one who did it all. Of course, I was with him; but it was his idea. That dirty rat did me in. If I ever get my hands on him, I'll take his cane and wrap it around his neck. It would be a pleasure doing time for something like that!"

"Hey, hey, Lori, don't get so uptight over him. You wouldn't want to do time for some stupid thing like that. I mean, baby, if you have to do time, do time for big things, not for a dirty weasel."

She had a point. It would be horrible to spend time in jail forever because of Cane Man.

She eased herself onto the bed beside me. Then she leaned over and whispered confidentially, "Lori, I can get you out of this place this afternoon. Interested?"

I backed away. "No way! I'm in enough trouble without adding an escape rap."

She giggled.

"Michelle, you've got to understand about this place. Someone told me that no girl has ever escaped from here. If you get out of the compound, you've got to climb a fence. After that, you have to swim the river. How do you think you could ever do all that?"

She giggled some more. "Nothing like that, Lori. Why, I can't even swim! And I'm not very good at climbing fences. What I've got in mind is easier than that—and it's all legit.

"A dear friend of mine will be here this afternoon to post bail for me. I'm telling you, kid, I'll be gone by two o'clock. You sound like a sweet kid who's had a bum rap. That mugging bail can't be too high. I just know my friend, who really loves me, would love you, too. I think he can get you out on bail."

"Come on, Michelle, what's the gimmick?"

"No gimmick. Honest."

"You're the first person I've met who's interested in helping me get out of this place. There's got to be a gimmick."

Michelle stood up. "Listen, Lori, there is absolutely no gimmick. My boyfriend, Lawrence Amour, is on the level. He just happens to be a very rich kid. He collects girls the way some guys collect stamps. I mean, when I tell him about how beautiful you are, you'll be on your way out of here just like that." She snapped her fingers. "I just know he's really going to love you."

I looked at her closely. Was there anything to this? Certainly no person alive would bail me out without even knowing me! There just had to be an angle.

Michelle started to walk away. I jumped up and grabbed her arm. Gimmick or no gimmick, I was interested.

"Listen, Michelle, I don't know what your game is, but I'm not going to rot in a place like this. Are you sure you can get me out, legit?"

"Well, sweetheart, I'll have to check with Lawrence first. At your arraignment some kind of bail must have been set. The bail for mugging old ladies can't be that much. By the way, doll, how long have you been mugging old ladies?"

"What do you mean, how long? This is the only time I've ever done anything like that."

"Have you got a previous record?"

"Of course not!" I answered indignantly. "So help me, Michelle, this is the first time. I can't even understand prisons or jails. I did it, but so help me the first time is also going to be the last time."

"Do you know how much your bail was?"

"Yes, a thousand bucks."

"Hey, sweetheart, I think this will be easy. I know Lawrence will really love you. I'm sure he'll bail you out."

"No strings attached?"

"No strings attached."

The prospect of getting out really lifted my spirits.

"Okay, Michelle, then I'm all for it. Something still sounds fishy, but I'll trust you."

"Baby, you can trust me more than you can trust your own mother!"

"Trust my mother? Michelle, if you only knew how much I hate her. That's not much of a comparison!"

"Aha! You have problems with your mother, too? Almost all of my friends have mother problems or father problems. But we all stick together, baby, and we make it!"

I started to ask what she meant by that, but she turned and walked away. "Okay, baby, see you later on this afternoon!" she called back.

I stretched out on my cot, wishing the hours away. *Free!* The word sounded so good. I could sympathize with anything in a cage. Free is what you want to be.

Sure enough, at about two o'clock the matron came for Michelle. Then at about three o'clock she came for me.

"Good news, Lori," she said. "Someone's bailed you out. You must have a guardian angel around."

I jumped off the bed and followed the matron into a little office where another woman sat. She had a few things for me to sign, and then they were through. They led me down a hall into a waiting room. There stood Michelle, grinning at me. Next to her stood a tall and very good looking man. *That must be Lawrence Amour,* I thought.

Michelle threw her arms around me. Then she said, "Lori, this is the man you can thank for your freedom. Lawrence, this is Lori Hutton."

Lawrence looked at me. "Oh," he said, "you're even more gorgeous than Michelle described. You are a *beautiful* girl!"

That felt good. I guess every girl likes to hear things like that.

Then he grabbed me and hugged me. I wasn't quite prepared for that. *But, after all,* I told myself, *he set me free. I guess I owe him something.*

Free! It was exhilarating to be a free woman. I vowed I'd do anything to keep from being cooped up in a jail again.

Outside we crossed the parking lot and stopped at the biggest, sleekest car on the lot. Lawrence opened the passenger door and motioned for me to get in the front. Michelle got in back.

I looked around. Crushed velvet upholstery. So luxurious. Every convenience. I guess it was the biggest, most beautiful car I had ever seen.

When he started the engine, I could hardly hear it. We drove out the entrance of the prison and across a bridge to the city.

I saw people turn and stare at us. I felt so proud. Yes,

Lawrence had to be very wealthy. I'd heard about these rich young men in New York City. And now I had met one. His dad probably owned a big company in Manhattan. Maybe he lived on a huge estate on Long Island. Maybe he was even taking me there!

But why? That question kept haunting me. I knew I must be living in a dream world, but it seemed like heaven.

I turned around to face Michelle. "Hey," I said, "I had no idea it would be like this! This is absolutely fantastic!"

Lawrence beamed. "All that I have, Lori, belongs to you and Michelle."

"Michelle, I can't believe this is happening to poor little Lori Hutton," I said. "It seems like a dream. Why, this car is so fancy, it looks like what I've heard the kids call a pimpmobile!"

Michelle's face turned white. She turned and stared out the window. Lawrence was strangely silent, too.

Had I said something wrong?

SEVEN

It didn't take me long to figure out where we were—in the middle of Manhattan.

"Hey, what are we doing here?"

"Lawrence had to pay a bundle to bail us out, Lori, so we have to do a little business to get the money back. Right, Lawrence?"

He just laughed.

"What kind of business are you in, Lawrence?"

"I'm involved in the oldest profession in the world," he answered with a knowing grin.

"Oldest profession?"

"Yes. You might call it buying and selling—or maybe selling and buying. But let's just say that we sell a product that always satisfies."

"Lawrence, you're a riot!" Michelle laughed.

I knew I was being taken in by something, but I was still pretty naive, and I couldn't figure out what was so funny.

"Okay, if you two are going to play games, let me do a little guessing."

Lawrence sobered. "Now, Lori, if you think it's bank

robbing, murdering, mugging, stealing, graft, corruption, or any of those things, I might as well put you straight right now."

"Don't tell me you're mixed up in the Mob!"

"No. It's a service business."

"Service business? What in the world is a service business?" They both burst out laughing, and I was getting a little upset by it all.

"Come on, you two. Why all the laughing? You're not trying to string me up to something that's bad, are you?"

The only answer I got was more laughter.

We now were driving slowly along Forty-second Street. Lawrence kept turning his head from one side to the other. What was he looking for? All I could see was the dirty street and a bunch of people milling around.

"Hey, Michelle!" He called out. "Look over there! There's Benny Atkins!"

"Hooray! Benny won't believe this when I tell him. I mean, Lawrence, that guy has got money—really big money."

"I know, baby! In fact, last night he was asking for you. I told him you got busted. But now he's ready—and probably with a fat wallet."

We quickly pulled to the curb. I still didn't have any answers, but it was becoming clearer that there was an angle to my freedom. I should have known that nobody does you a favor without expecting something in return.

Michelle jumped out of the backseat and took off in search of Benny Atkins. Then Lawrence reached across me, opened my door, and pushed me out.

I looked at him, puzzled. He smiled that big smile. "Remember, little girl," he said, "if it weren't for me, you'd still be rotting in that jail cell—and for no telling how long!"

I was half-in and half-out of the car. Michelle came back and pulled me the rest of the way out. "Listen, kid," she whispered, "you're about to face the moment of truth. I'm going to introduce you to Benny. He wants your services, and you'd better go along with it. If you make any mistakes, it will be your neck—and I mean your neck." She ran her finger across her neck menacingly.

Suddenly it hit me full force. "Service business!" So that was it. They had trapped me into prostitution. I should have known when Michelle told me she was in for pros!

No way was I going to be involved in something like this. But Michelle must have read my mind, for before I could react she grabbed my wrist and twisted it behind me. "Lori, I'm not playing games. Look at my other hand."

A switchblade! And pointing at my stomach!

"One false move, kid, and they'll find your body in some back alley."

My heart raced wildly. So this was their game! Lawrence Amour was a pimp. He had probably let Michelle get arrested so she could go into prison overnight and recruit naive idiots like me! Of course I wanted out of jail. Of course I was cut off from my parents. But I certainly didn't bargain to be a prostitute. The very thought of it nauseated me.

Michelle whirled me around and marched me toward Benny Atkins. The switchblade still pointed at me menacingly.

"Hey, Benny," Michelle called. "You're sure looking good. How have you been?"

"Hey, Michelle baby, you're looking good, too—I mean really good. I missed you last night!" Michelle threw her arms around him, drawing her body very close to his.

This was my chance!

I took off as fast as I could. About twenty feet away I glanced over my shoulder. Michelle and Benny were just standing there, watching me. This was going to be easier than I had thought. I could get lost in this crowd. . . .

Just then I felt a strong arm encircle my waist. Something swept me off my feet, and I struggled to get free. My arms and legs beat the air wildly—and futilely.

"Hey, baby, where are you going so fast?" Lawrence had me. I thought he had driven off. He must have expected me to try something like this.

I was still kicking as he carried me back to the car, opened the door, and shoved me inside. People all around us were laughing. They probably knew who he was and what was happening. But it sure wasn't funny to me!

He shoved me in farther and got in beside me. Grabbing my hand, he squeezed hard on my little finger, forcing it away from the others. I thought the pain would kill me.

"Now listen, little girl. You'd better just stay cool, do you understand? I didn't put any thousand bucks to bail you out just to be kind to a poor little kid. All I want is to get my money back—with interest. Do you hear?"

I just sat there. He let go of my finger. Apparently he had decided on another approach.

"You and me, Lori—we've got a chance to make it big—and I mean big. Michelle is setting it up for you. Benny's a gentle man, and he won't hurt you. He pays well, so that will help get the bail money paid back."

I knew what Lawrence was telling me. He was

peddling my body. That was thoroughly disgusting, and I wanted no part of it.

When I didn't answer, he grabbed my finger again and squeezed harder. "Ouch!" I yelled. "That really hurts!"

"Listen, kid, squeezing your little finger is just the first thing. Either you cooperate, or I'm going to squeeze your pretty little neck until your eyes bug out. Then I'm going to take my switchblade and cut you up into tiny little pieces and throw them all in the Hudson River for the fish to eat. Now either you cooperate, or you'll be fish bait. What's it going to be?"

Choice? What choice did I have? I remembered hearing about a pimp throwing a teenage girl out a window because she wouldn't cooperate. These pimps meant business—and I sure didn't want to end up as fish food!

"Okay, you win. Let go of my finger, and I'll do it this one time. But this is going to be the last! Do you understand?"

"Listen, baby, I'll make a deal with you. This can be the last time, if you really want it that way. After you get through with Benny, you can do what you want. Is it a deal?"

I didn't know pimps made deals. Maybe this wouldn't be so bad, after all.

"Okay, it's a deal. But how do I know Benny won't hurt me? I mean, I've read stories about how some of these guys kill prostitutes."

"You leave Benny to me," Lawrence purred. "Benny knows me, and I know Benny, and Benny knows my girls. A lot of people in Times Square know me and my girls. If anybody messes with my girls, they don't mess with anybody after that!"

Lawrence helped me out of the car just as Michelle and Benny walked up.

"Goodness, Michelle, you were absolutely right! This *is* a cute little number. You say she's the best in town?"

"She's the best, Benny!" Then she whispered something to Lawrence. His face lit up. He must have gotten a good price for me.

"Okay, you two," Lawrence said, "just walk off down the street and have a good time. And so help me, Benny, if you try to kidnap her, I'll put you away for a hundred years!"

The three of them laughed, but I didn't. I was scared to death!

Benny grabbed my arm and led me away. He tried to make conversation. "I understand you're a friend of Michelle and Lawrence's. Is that right?"

This was the way people treated friends? I didn't answer.

"Michelle was telling me that you don't have anybody left in the world. I guess your mother and father have cut you off. Is that what happened?"

Michelle must have given him a real sob story. But the sad part was, it was true. I'd do anything to keep from going back to jail, and I couldn't go back home. No one really cared what happened to me.

I was so wrapped up with my thoughts and fears that Benny didn't say anything else as we walked the three blocks to his apartment.

Inside his room I immediately took off all my clothes. I was embarrassed beyond belief, but I knew I had no choice. Somehow I had to figure a way to get out of the clutches of Lawrence and Michelle. I really didn't trust his "deal." I figured that as soon as I got through with this one, there would be another. And another.

And another. The whole situation was so disgusting. I had to get out now!

When I started to leave Benny's hotel room, he called, "Not so fast, Lori. I promised Michelle and Lawrence I'd bring you right back. In fact, I had to pay a deposit of two hundred dollars. Can you imagine anything like that?"

Well, maybe I did have some value—at least two hundred dollars. But the idea of paying a deposit on me—like on a soft-drink bottle! How low had I sunk?

"Now, Lori, if I don't bring you back, I lose two hundred dollars. And Lawrence also said something about the fish in the Hudson River being hungry. What do you suppose he meant by that? Well, I know one thing for sure; there isn't any way you're going to escape from me. So please don't try anything. Okay?"

"What do you mean, 'try anything'? I'm just as afraid of Lawrence and Michelle as you are."

There had to be some way out of this mess. Maybe if I could call my dad and he knew he didn't have to pay my bail, he would reconsider. That's when a plan hit me!

"Mr. Atkins, did you enjoy your time with me?"

His eyes lit up. "You'd better believe it. That was absolutely fantastic!"

"Well, if you think that was good, I've got a sister at home. She's even better."

"Better than you? You're kidding!" His eyes bugged.

"That isn't all, Mr. Atkins. I don't know how much Michelle told you about me, but I have the worst homelife imaginable, and this is the absolute truth. My old man's a gangster, and my old lady's a nut. Living at home has been hell on earth. I had decided it would be better to spend my life in jail, but my good friend

Michelle talked to me. Lawrence interceded, and I was able to get out. But you have no idea how much my sister, Peggy, wants out. Why, if I just made a phone call to her, she'd come running right away. And Lawrence wouldn't be in on the deal!"

By this time Benny was jumping up and down with excitement.

"And that isn't all, Mr. Atkins. You can have her for free!"

"Oh, wow! Wow! This is too good to believe! Wait until the boys hear about this! When can she come?"

"Right now. All I have to do is use your phone to call her."

"Sure! Sure! The phone's right over there."

I sat down and dialed the number. Somehow I had to bluff my way through this one. I had no idea what I was going to say, but at least I'd gotten as far as the telephone.

I dialed the number and waited. It rang and rang. Someone had to be home!

I glanced up at Benny. He had a smile like you wouldn't believe. I guess he really liked young girls.

Just then I heard the click and Peggy's voice.

"Peggy, this is Lori."

"Lori!" she screamed. "Where are you?"

"I'm in the middle of Manhattan. I've met some fantastic people who are really interested in me. One of them even bailed me out of jail. These people are going to care for me for the rest of my life. You wouldn't believe the place I'm staying in. I mean, it is absolutely gorgeous. It's a twelve-room apartment, and the people are so wonderful to me. I never dreamed I'd end up in a place like this."

"Lori, is this another of your big stories?"

"Peggy, would I lie to you? Here, if you don't belive me, you can talk to the man of the house. I'm just sitting here having coffee with Mr. Schoenberg."

I knew Benny was eager enough to play along. "Hello, Peggy. Yes, this is Mr. Schoenberg. I just wanted to tell you what a lovely person your sister, Lori, is. Mrs. Schoenberg and I have fallen in love with her, and she can stay with us forever. What do you think of that?"

Now I was in a trap. I couldn't tell Peggy I was in this sex fiend's apartment. I grabbed the receiver away from Benny. He was all smiles.

"Peggy, is Dad around somewhere?"

"Yes, just a minute. But I can tell you that he's still furious with you. That deal with the old lady was in all of the papers. Dad went down to the hospital to visit her. Would you believe he got her to drop all the charges? She said she won't even show up in court. I guess you can thank your lucky boots that nothing is going to happen to you now."

I couldn't get over it. I was getting off free. I really didn't owe Lawrence anything. If only I had waited in jail for another few days. Now maybe I could go home—if I could get out of the clutches of Michelle, Lawrence, and Benny Atkins.

"Hang on, just a minute. I'll get Dad for you."

I put my hand over the mouthpiece and whispered, "Mr. Atkins, my dad's going to get on the phone, and I want to tell him something privately. Please trust me. I'll tell you what it is later, but I'm too embarrassed to tell my father in front of you. Okay?"

"I'll just turn my back and plug my ears."

"No! No! Please go into the bathroom and shut the door. I promise I'll just be a couple of minutes. Okay?"

"No way. While I'm in the bathroom, you'll take off."

Just then I heard Dad's voice. "For crying out loud, Mr. Atkins. Can't you trust me?"

"No way!"

Dad was yelling into the receiver. I had to think of something quickly or he would hang up.

"Okay, Benny, then step out in the hallway. I'm certainly not going to jump out the window. And you'd better do as I say, or Peggy's not coming!"

He turned and headed for the door. I lifted my hand from the mouthpiece. "Dad?"

"Lori, I've heard all the nonsense I want to hear from you! What do you want? And make it quick!"

"Please, Dad, I'm out of jail, but I'm still in trouble. I really need you to get me out!"

"What do you mean, get you out?" he yelled. "As far as I'm concerned, you *are* out—out of my life—out of your mother's life—out of Peggy's life. Ever since you left this house, we've had peace. I already did you a big favor with that old lady. You'd better be thankful that you're not going to rot in jail for the rest of your life!"

"Dad, I don't know how to tell you how much I appreciate that. But I'm in a really big jam, and I need help. Can you help me?"

"Can I help you?" he yelled. "Yes, I can help you. I can help you by telling you never to call again! Don't ever show up in this neighborhood! I've been embarrassed, humiliated, and scoffed at because of the terrible things you've done. People are whispering behind my back everywhere. My sales have dropped off to almost zero because of you. To think my own daughter would almost kill a helpless old lady to get a few bucks. This is one of the most horrible things I have ever had to face. Lori, I don't ever want to see or hear from you again. Good-bye!"

He slammed the receiver so hard it almost deafened me. I choked back a sob and hung up the receiver. Now it was really clear. There was no way out.

Benny was standing at the door, all excited. "Sorry, Mr. Atkins. Peggy has a boyfriend. They're getting married next week."

"You're kidding. Why so soon?"

"She just wants to get out of the house. But she said he's a great guy. Tough luck."

"Yes, tough luck," he murmured.

"Okay, you can take me back to Lawrence now."

He was waiting for us, and he tried to look mean. I called his bluff. "Okay, Lawrence, just cool it. You don't need to make any threats. You don't need to throw me into the Hudson River—and you don't need to take me back to jail."

"What?" he exclaimed. "What are you talking about?"

"Okay, I'll say it right out front. I am never, never, never going home again!"

He was beaming.

"Okay, lead me to the next customer."

"Hey, baby, this is too good to be true. Believe me, you and I are going to make enough money to build a huge castle on Long Island!"

Then he reached into his pocket and handed me something: a switchblade.

"You carry that at all times, baby. One day you'll need it."

It wasn't too long before that prophecy came true.

EIGHT

Michelle filled me in on the world of prostitution. She showed me the best corners to hang out and where to take the "tricks," as we called the customers.

And when we were alone, she also told me about Lawrence. As far as she knew, he had never really hurt any of his girls, but he always made big threats. But she said she wasn't about to cross him because one never knew about these pimps. If they ever exploded, somebody would probably be killed—and she didn't intend for that somebody to be her!

She told me how much to charge the tricks, or "johns" as she sometimes called them. I found out there was no set rate; she simply tried to get as much as she could. And it was always a cash business—cash before the business.

Michelle warned me never to make myself cheap. Under no circumstances was I to charge less than twenty-five dollars. Since I was so young, I should be able to get one hundred dollars. Some of these characters were looking for younger girls, she said, and they were willing to pay. Therefore, I was to try to get two hundred dollars or even three hundred dollars.

We walked together to a hotel that she used on

Forty-sixth Street. The guy at the desk knew what it was all about. Whenever we used a room, Lawrence would come by later and pay for it. That guy also knew how to keep the cops away.

As we walked back to Forty-second Street, I asked her how much we made on these deals. "Is it fifty-fifty?"

She laughed at that. "You really haven't been around much, have you, kid? No, it's not that kind of a business with Lawrence. As I told you, he takes good care of us. We stay in his expensive apartment, and he satisfies all our needs—I mean, every single one of them. So you just turn all the money over to Lawrence. You won't need any money."

"What do you mean, turn all the money over to him? Do you mean I do all the work and he gets all the money? That's not right. I'm not going to work that way!"

"Listen, kid, don't be so quick to shoot off your mouth. Look at it this way. Just suppose that you say to Lawrence that you're not going to give him one dime. Then what?"

I thought about it. Where could I go? I certainly couldn't go home.

"Do you see what I mean? You really can't do anything else. I mean, I guess you could get yourself a hotel room for the night, but you'd better believe Lawrence would come looking for you. So it's really like robbing Lawrence because he's the one who's looking out for you and your interests. Lawrence is feeding you, giving you a bed to sleep in, and taking care of all of your personal needs. He'll dress you up like a doll, and you'll get to ride all over town in his Rolls. Believe me, baby, you can't ask for more than that, can you?"

She was right. I really had no one else I could turn to. I guess he had me. So I decided I'd better cooperate and get along as best I could.

One Saturday night business was booming. I had already taken three different guys to the hotel room.

At about eleven o'clock I was standing on the corner of Forty-third and Eight Avenue when two very tall, macho guys came up and propositioned me. From their appearance I could tell they had a lot of money, so when they asked me how much I charged, I said, "Two hundred dollars."

One of the guys smiled. "Just two hundred dollars?"

I looked him over. Maybe I should have asked for four hundred dollars!

"Now let me get this straight," he said. "You're asking for two hundred dollars. Is that each or is that for both of us?"

"That's two hundred dollars each."

"Okay. No sweat. This will really be worth it!"

"Let's go on up to Forty-sixth Street," I said.

We got to Forty-fifth Street and were passing a very expensive car when one of them said, "Hey, sweetheart, if you don't mind, why don't we get into our car here and go over by the river. I've got a wife and two kids at home, and I'm scared to death that if the cops broke into the hotel and we got caught in the act, my career would be ruined. I mean my whole business would go down the tubes. You wouldn't mind using our car, would you?"

I looked at both of them, and then I looked at the car. Everything seemed to be on the level.

"Oh, I guess it's okay. But at the price I quoted you, it will have to be quick. I don't have time to go driving off into the countryside looking at the moon."

"I'll tell you what," one of them said. "We'll just drive over to the docks on Fifty-seventh Street. There's no one around there at this time of night. It'll just take a few minutes to drive there."

"Okay. But if it takes too long, the price goes up." He opened the door for me, and I got into the front seat. I slid over, thinking that the other guy would get in beside me. But no, he got into the back. Strange. I hoped I wasn't making a mistake by doing this. After all, nobody knew where I was.

As soon as we drove away, the driver lit up some pot and handed it to me. I took a big drag. Maybe this would make things easier.

The guy was right. In minutes we were at Fifty-seventh Street on the West Side. All I could see were a bunch of dilapidated, run-down docks. They looked as though they hadn't been used in years.

We drove off the blacktop and bounced along a dirt road, finally stopping in front of what looked like an old warehouse. Dim lights cast an eerie glow. Not a soul stirred anywhere.

Water splashed against the docks, rhythmically breaking the silence of the place. Why, oh why had I ever let them talk me into coming down to this godforsaken place? Even if they were on the level, there was no telling what was lurking in the shadows or in that warehouse!

By this time the guys had finished the pot and were giddy.

I sneaked a glance at the driver. He flashed a big smile. Just then the guy in the backseat leaned forward. I felt his big hand on my shoulder. I sensed something was coming.

I wrenched myself free and half-turned to face them both. "Okay, you guys, I don't know what you're up to, but let me give it to you straight. If you lay one hand on me, I'll pull my switchblade and slash somebody's throat!"

I figured I might as well get tough with them now. Nobody was going to fool around with me!

"Do you understand what I'm talking about?" I said it with more courage than I had at the moment.

Then, click! I knew what that was! Too late for me to go for my switchblade now, for his was already at my neck.

"Okay, little girl, now you listen. You slide out of this car and do as we say. One peep out of you, and my switchblade will plunge into your heart, and they'll find you in the river in the morning. Now move!"

I sat there, too scared to do anything. Then, click! The driver whipped out his switchblade and jabbed me in the ribs.

"Ouch, you dumb nut! That thing hurt me!"

He laughed as though that were the funniest thing he had heard all day. Then he said, "Okay, little girl, you heard what the man said. Now move!" Then he jabbed me again.

The one in the backseat was outside by my door. "Okay, slide out real easy," the driver said. "My partner, Amos, is out there waiting for you, and I'll be right behind you. One false move, and you'll have two switchblades in your back—and I mean *deep*. Now move!"

Without any real choice I slid out. I eased my feet to the dirt road and raised myself up slowly. I didn't want either of them to interpret any move I made as "false"!

I'd heard about this kind before. They're tough guys, usually with prison records, and they're not afraid of anyone or anything. They pick up young girls such as me with one thing in mind: rape!

In our talks together, Michelle had warned me about rapists. Usually after they raped a girl, they mutilated her body with their knives. There was something animalistic about rapists, she said. They hate women, and with sadistic vengeance they often kill their victims. Something flashed through my mind about a young girl whose hands were cut off by a rapist—but she lived.

Terrified, I glanced around. I was on totally unfamiliar turf. *Maybe somebody will see us*, I thought. Then I could scream for help. But who would help me when two big men stood there with switchblades?

I remembered a story about a girl who was being murdered, and thirty-eight people heard her cries for help. No one answered. And that was right here in New York City.

In the distance I saw car lights. Then, miracle of miracles, the car seemed to turn and head straight for us! Maybe this was my chance.

Amos saw it, too. He twisted my arm behind my back and jabbed his switchblade into my ribs. "Okay, girl, if you try anything funny, you're a dead duck." Then he said to his partner, "Randy, you cover us."

Randy yanked open the glove compartment and pulled out a pistol. "This could be some cops," he said. "I don't plan to go back to the slammer."

He flicked a little switch on the side of the pistol, and the magazine with bullets slipped out. "It's full. I can really blast away if anyone tries anything." Then he crawled underneath the car.

Those headlights got closer and closer. Apparently they were coming where we were. I couldn't believe all that was happening. I was about to be raped, and now I was going to be in the middle of a shoot-out.

Amos reached into my blouse to look for my switchblade. Then he reached into the back pocket of my jeans. He grabbed the knife and flipped it into the river. There went what little defense I had.

As the car came closer, Amos wheeled me around

and threw his arms around me. He started kissing me. I tried to pull away.

"Listen, kid, you start kissing me passionately," he commanded. "I don't know who's in that car, but if it's cops, I'm going to get out of here even if we have to shoot our way out. Now cooperate, or you're going to be the first one to go!"

I threw my arms around Amos and tried to act as realistic as I could. I wasn't about to get myself killed.

We broke from the kiss, and Amos said, "Okay, grab my hand and start walking away from our car. When that other car gets up beside us, you throw your arms around me and kiss me again!"

It was dark I could hardly see where to walk. Just then the car pulled up alongside us, and a spotlight pierced the darkness, temporarily blinding us. But I could make out the identification on the doors. Cops!

"Hey, what are you two doing down here?"

"Well, hello there, officer," Amos answered. "My little bride and I have just driven into New York City for our honeymoon. We heard about how romantic the Hudson River was, and we decided to come down here and smooch a little."

"Well, buddy, you can get yourself hurt down here."

Amos drew his body close to mine. "Okay, girl, grab me and start kissing. And make it for real!"

I pushed my lips against his and wiggled my head back and forth as passionately as I could. I heard the officers laugh. Amos broke away. "Do you see what I mean, officer? My bride just had to go through with that kiss, police officers or no police officers."

Then he growled in my ear, "You do exactly as I say, and we'll get out of this." I glanced back toward Amos's car. I could just barely make out the other guy's form underneath it. It looked as though his gun was aimed right at me.

We walked up beside the police car, and the officer rolled down his window. "Well, young lady, I guess you're going to have a lot to tell the folks back home, aren't you?"

I faked a weak smile.

"Officer," Amos said, "back in our hometown in Pennsylvania, the people read about your policemen here in New York City. They think you're a bunch of bad guys. But I know differently. I can tell you two are real gentlemen. You certainly wouldn't take bribes or anything like that."

Amos had those cops eating out of his hand. But what in the world was he up to? "Now, officer, my little bride here has told my brother that when she came to New York City, she was going to find a cop and kiss him."

The officers laughed. "Now, officer, if I promise not to tell your wife, would you mind if my wife gave you a little kiss? I mean, it will be absolutely hilarious when Jacqueline gets home and tells our friends she kissed a New York City policeman!"

Without any further encouragement the officer poked his head out of the window and puckered. I knew that pistol was still aimed at me. I kissed the officer.

"Wow! That was absolutely fantastic!" he exclaimed. "Some days it really pays to be a police officer in New York City!"

Amos laughed. I tried to, but very little came out. Then the other officer jumped out of the car and came running over. Did he suspect something? Would he pull his gun?

"Hey, you're not being fair!" he told me. "If my partner gets a kiss, then I do, too!" I could see there was no way around this one. I had to kiss this officer, too.

"Okay, Jacqueline, you're going to tell the folks back home that you kissed two police officers!"

This officer was young, and not bad looking. Then something hit me. I would grab him and kiss him passionately. Then I would grab his gun and turn it on Amos before the guy under the car could see what was happening. Maybe I could get out of this jam, after all.

I ran toward the young officer and threw my arms around him. That must have surprised him, for he acted as if he weren't sure what to do. I kissed him as passionately as I could, and he really got to enjoying it. He squeezed me tight and hung on. So did I.

Then I felt his grip around me tighten. He was really enjoying it. I moved my hands around his back, getting lower and lower and feeling around for the end of the gun. Then I touched it.

I started to give it a quick jerk, but then I felt a hand over mine. I opened my eyes. Amos must have guessed what I was up to and grabbed my hand. Dirty luck.

So the policeman wouldn't suspect what was going on, Amos said, "Hey! Hey! Break it up, you two. I agreed to a kiss, Jacqueline, but not this. You're making me jealous!"

I backed away from the officer. He stood there, sort of dazed. "My, my! I certainly wish all the tourists were like this! I'd work for the police department for nothing!" Everybody laughed but me.

Amos threw his arm around my shoulders and pulled me toward him. "Nice try, kid, but you blew it!" he whispered. "I saw you go for the gun. Now one peep out of you, and I'll jam this switchblade into your heart—and my buddy over there will let those two nice cops have it. So keep still!"

Then he spoke to the police. "Well, officers, I'm afraid that's the limit on the kisses."

"Sir," one of them said, "you don't know how lucky you are. You have a fantastic bride. I wish you much success."

The other one agreed. Then he added, "But, sir, I would advise you to get back to your hotel room. Every so often we find people down in this part of town who are up to no good. I don't want to scare you or anything, but every few days we pull a body out of this river. Sometimes it's an old man; sometimes a young girl. In fact, that's why we came down here. We thought maybe something was wrong. We always check out any cars down here. So you'd better get back to your hotel right away. Okay?"

"Yes, sir," Amos responded. "In fact, we're going to walk over to the car and head back right now." With that, the officers drove off, leaving us standing there.

As soon as they were out of sight, Amos lifted his huge hand and stung me across the face. "You filthy little prostitute!" he screamed. "You thought you were smart, didn't you?"

I fell back, trying to keep my balance on the uneven road. "I ought to do you in right now!" he yelled. "Don't you know that if my buddy and I got busted, they'd send us straight back up the river? And, baby, the second time means years. Lots of years. You don't know how lucky you are to be alive!"

He twisted my arm behind me again and pushed me past the car. "Come on, Randy," he called out. "Let's go over to that vacant warehouse and get this over with."

Randy crawled out from under the car, still carrying the pistol. I stumbled ahead of them to the warehouse.

The creaky, old door yielded easily to Randy's kick. They pushed me inside and waited for a minute while they sized up the situation. I couldn't see very far, but it looked as though the place was totally deserted. All I could hear was water slapping against the pilings. The wood smelled rotten. I worried that our weight might cause the whole thing to fall into the river. Talk about a spooky, scary place.

Apparently assured that no one else was around, the two guys turned toward me. I knew what was coming. Maybe I could still talk my way out of it.

"Okay, you guys, I'll tell you what. I'll make a deal with you. Forget about the two hundred bucks. You can have it for free. Okay?"

Almost before the words were out of my mouth, Amos grabbed my blouse and gave it a quick jerk. Buttons popped everywhere. Then his foot went behind my legs, and with a quick shove he had me down on those filthy planks and was right on top of me. I screamed at the top of my lungs.

Randy dropped to his knees and put his hand over my mouth. That shut me up, but I started kicking with all my might.

"We've got us a little tiger here, Randy. Come on. Let's tame her!"

Amos grabbed my blouse and stuffed it into my mouth. Randy grabbed my legs and then Amos pinned my arms flat on the bare planks. No way was I a match for those big bruisers!

I tried to scream, but no sound came out. I gasped for air because my nose couldn't bring it in fast enough. My heart beat wildly. Then they ripped off the rest of my clothing and pounded on me like a couple of animals.

I absolutely cannot tell how I felt. The pain was unbelievable. I was utterly humiliated and frustrated and so angry that I would have killed both of them in a minute if I could have done so. Murder wouldn't be good enough for two beasts like them.

They both got what they wanted and then stood there staring at me, as if trying to decide what to do with me now.

Would you believe they started laughing? "Well, little tiger, are you a little tamer now?" Randy asked derisively. Then he booted me in the side.

I writhed in pain, my muffled screams echoing through the vacant warehouse and coming back to taunt me.

I knew the next thing was more torture until finally, death. But when my agony eased a little and I looked around, I realized I was alone. I hadn't heard the car drive away. Maybe it was stolen and they had left it—or maybe they were waiting outside to attack me again.

I pulled the blouse out of my mouth and tried to get some air to my lungs. I was so exhausted from the ordeal and hurt so much that I didn't even get up.

I thought of all the terrible events of my life that had led up to this horrible nightmare. Wasn't there some way out? What was the use of living, anyway? And why was I being singled out by fate to suffer so?

Tears gushed down my cheeks, and I couldn't help but think once again that the only way out was to kill myself. Through my sobs I heard those persistent waters hitting the pilings. Why not let the Hudson River claim one more life? Who would care?

I don't know how long I lay there sobbing, but finally I rolled over and got on my knees. I almost passed out from the pain, but I crawled around and located the rest of my clothing, piece by piece.

As I got my clothes on, I began to figure I'd better take my chances outside. No one would find me in here.

I half-crawled to the door and pushed it open a crack. Good! The car was gone. At least they weren't lurking in the shadows somewhere!

I pulled myself to my feet and stepped into the night air. Now what? Back to Times Square and Lawrence? Would he take care of me? Sure, but there was bound to be another night like this one—and probably next time the rapists would finish me off.

I stumbled along the road toward Fifty-seventh Street. Every step was sheer agony, and I stopped frequently. Then I glanced up and saw car lights heading toward me. All I could think was that it must be Amos and Randy. Maybe they had had second thoughts about leaving me alive. After all, I did know their names. Yes, that was it! They were coming back to kill me!

Well, after what I had been through, I wasn't about to let them get their hands on me again. They wanted to kill me, did they? Well, I would just beat them to it!

I turned and headed toward the end of the dock. They had spotted me, and the lights kept coming faster and faster. They were headed out onto the dock after me.

At the end of the dock I turned around for one second. The car screeched to a halt. I saw a door fly open.

Then in one split second I looked at the river. The water seemed so black and cold. But there was no turning back now. It was death either way, and I wasn't about to be cut in little pieces by two maniacs.

They were running toward me. Not much time. Now!

I grabbed my nose and jumped. The waters swallowed me quickly. Death was near. I tried to accept that, but something within me wouldn't quit without a struggle. I began to flail with my arms.

But was it too late?

NINE

I felt my face break through the surface of the river the first time. Almost simultaneously I felt a strong arm around my neck. Oh, no! Amos had jumped in after me. Now he was trying to choke me! Why couldn't he just let me die?

I grabbed wildly for his eyes. If I could scratch them, he'd have to let go of me! Kicking and flailing, I felt myself slip under the water again.

But that strong arm around my neck wouldn't let go. Up I came again. Then, smack! He hit me right between the eyes. All feeling drained from my body. Instinctively I knew that in another few minutes it would all be over. Then in a few days my body would float to the surface. Another victim. . . .

I gasped for breath. In the darkness I could see that fist coming again. I tried to ward it off, but it was too late. Then—nothing. . . .

The next thing I remember was the pressure of my cheek against a plank of the dock. Somebody seemed to be on top of me. With what little strength I had I called out in terror, "Please! Please! Please! Don't do it again! I can't stand it again!"

"Hey, Todd, she's coming to!"

Todd? Who was Todd? Where was I? What was going on?

With great effort I opened my eyes. There in the glare of the spotlight I saw friendly faces—those two cops!

"What happened?" I coughed.

"Are you kidding? I dove into that filthy water to save your neck, and you tried to kill me! The tide was so swift it pulled us underneath the docks among all those pilings. I almost got killed trying to rescue you. You sure didn't make it very easy!"

"Oh, I'm sorry. Please forgive me. I guess I didn't realize what was happening. I had no idea it was you two."

"Come on, now, level with us," one of them said. "I thought you and your husband were heading back to your hotel. Did you have a big fight or something?"

"Okay, I'll tell you the truth. That wasn't my husband, and there was no fight. What really happened was that I was uptown in a restaurant having a cup of coffee, and these two guys walked up and propositioned me. Those two scums thought I was a prostitute. Man, I'm no prostitute. I'm just a plain, decent girl who lives in Queens. Under no circumstances would I bow to such filth."

"Okay, okay. Don't tell me you went out with those two guys?"

"Are you kidding? As soon as they tried to proposition me, I paid my bill and left. But those jerks followed me to the street. The next thing I knew one of them had a switchblade in my ribs. They forced me into their car and drove here. After you two left, they pushed me into that deserted warehouse, ripped off all my clothes, and, well, you can imagine what happened next."

"Are you sure you're telling the truth? How come you didn't try to get away when we came down here?"

"Listen, do you remember when you got out of the police car and came around for a kiss? Well, when I threw my arms around you and kissed you the way I did, I was trying to get your gun. I was going to shoot the one jerk and then fire at the other guy who was hiding under the car with a pistol aimed at me."

"Hey, lady, thank God you didn't try anything as stupid as that. If those two guys were up to no good, they wouldn't have stopped at anything."

"Well, officers, that was part of my problem. Those jerks have done time, and they said they weren't about to go back to prison. They threatened to shoot both of you if I tried anything. You wouldn't have had a chance."

"Okay, just rest now. We've got an ambulance on the way to take you to the hospital.

"And you can be glad we came back here to recheck. When that car drove out, we were down a block and saw two guys in the car. We thought something was fishy, so we decided to come back down here."

"Yes, but when I saw the headlights, I thought it was those two jerks coming back to finish me off. So I decided to try to swim to New Jersey. I couldn't live through another rape!"

"You were a tough one in the water," one of them said. "The more I tried to pull you out, the harder you struggled. Finally I had to knock you out!"

"I'm sorry, officer. If I had known it was you, I would have cooperated. I was just trying to save my own neck from those thugs, and—"

A siren interrupted my words. One of the officers ran to the patrol car and flipped the red light on. The ambulance driver must have spotted it, for he sped toward us.

How was I going to get out of this one? I really didn't want to go to the hospital—no telling what might happen from there.

"Sir, do I have to go to the hospital? I think I'm all right now. I'll just go back uptown and take a taxi back home. Is that okay?"

He laughed. "You're a brave little girl, but I think it's best that we admit you to the hospital. We have to fill out a report on all of this, and I'm still not totally convinced of your story. But the doctor will check you out. If you've been raped, he can tell us. And if you haven't been raped, we might have to book you on attempted suicide. Then you'll be kept for a few days for observation."

"For crying out loud, don't you believe a citizen of this country? I said I was raped. Look at my blouse! It's all torn apart. Any doctor will find I've been raped!"

The officer didn't answer, and before I could think of any more arguments, the two ambulance attendants gently slid me onto a stretcher and rushed me away.

The young intern at the emergency room took one quick look and knew I had been raped. He told me I was being kept overnight for observation. I don't know what the two officers told the doctors, but the more I objected to staying, the more they insisted. I decided it would be best to cooperate. Besides, the whole ordeal had left me pretty well drained physically and emotionally. This was also going to be a good opportunity to see if Lawrence really would take care of everything—such as hospital bills when one of his girls was raped.

The next afternoon I was released. My clothes had been washed and dried. Someone had even sewed some buttons on my blouse. I hadn't expected any kindnesses such as that.

For a few minutes I stood outside the hospital,

wondering what to do. In one way, I was free now. As far as I knew, Lawrence had no idea where I was. But where could I go? Certainly not home. I had no money—nothing but the clothes on my back. *I might as well admit I'm trapped*, I told myself, and I headed back to the apartment.

Michelle took one look at me when I walked in and yelled, "Lori! Whatever happened to you? We've been worried sick!"

"What do you mean, what happened? I just about got killed!"

"Oh, honey, your face is a mess. You look like you've tangled with a lion."

"That would have been easy if it had been an ordinary beast! Two maniacs forced me up to the West Side and into one of those deserted warehouses along the river. Both of them raped me! I thought I was a goner!"

"Uh-oh! Wait until Lawrence hears about this!"

Just then he walked into the living room. "Michelle, I thought I heard Lori, and. . . ." His voice trailed off as he looked at me.

"Lori! What happened?"

I rehearsed all the gory details. I needed all the sympathy I could get.

When he was sure I was through, he said, "As soon as I catch those guys, it'll be the last time they rape anybody—especially one of my girls!" With that he bolted from the apartment.

"Michelle, do you think he'll kill those guys?"

"Yes."

"Well, killing is too good for those animals. But he doesn't even know who they are! You don't think he'll knock off a couple of innocent guys, do you?"

"You mentioned Amos, Lori. Don't you know who Amos is?"

"No. I had never heard of the guy until last night."

"Well, Amos just got out of prison after doing ten years, and his partner, Randy, just got out, too."

"Hey," I interrupted, "that's right. He did call his partner Randy. I half-laughed when I heard it—Amos and Randy. But that was before...."

"Well," Michelle continued, "a couple of days ago they held up a bank in Jersey. I heard they bought a fancy new car. I know they've been flashing money all over Manhattan. Well, Amos used to be a pimp, and he's probably out looking for girls again. Lawrence had been watching him. I should have warned you."

"Do you mean that in a big, impersonal city like this, some people know all that's going on? I can't believe it!"

"The city may be big, but on the street everybody knows what everybody else is doing. We've got to—to survive. And street people have their own ways of communicating. When Amos came around, everybody knew he was up to something. The problem is, Amos picked the wrong girl. If he'd known you were Lawrence's girl, he would have avoided you! So too bad for Amos and Randy. They'll get what's coming to them, now!"

I slouched back into an easy chair, too exhausted to talk anymore. But I couldn't shut my mind off.

I couldn't believe I was getting so deep into prostitution and crime in such a short time. Not only was *I* almost killed, but because of me two other people were going to be killed.

Then I wondered what would happen if Lawrence tried to kill those guys and muffed it. Would Amos and Randy come looking for me to settle the score? They'd have no mercy, now!

Maybe I was too tired to talk, but Michelle kept rattling on like an old mother hen. I knew she felt somewhat responsible for the mess I was in.

"Now the next time a couple of guys grab you and try something, Lori, you start screaming that you are Lawrence's girl. It may not always help, but it could save your neck. Yell anything.

"I remember once I yelled that I was an undercover cop. You should have seen that guy take off!

"And another thing, Lori. You'd better get smarter with that switchblade. Don't ever bluff with it. Use it!

"One time I had to stab a guy. He screamed like a stuck pig. I don't know whether or not he died, but at least I'm still alive. You'd better wise up, Lori, if you want to survive!"

I got more and more fidgety, sitting there. I felt so dirty. Even the clothes I had on reminded me of that unspeakable experience.

"Michelle, I've just got to change. I can't stand the sight of this blouse. I feel so horrible."

She followed me into my bedroom. "Well, you'd better get into something and hit the street as soon as possible. Things have been a little slow, and Lawrence is getting uptight. When you didn't come back last night, he really went into a tizzy. He thought you had taken off. So you'd better go out and hit the street to show your loyalty."

"No, Michelle, no! Don't you understand? I just got raped! It was brutal! I've got to have some rest! I couldn't stand the pain!"

"I'm sorry, kid, but you have to learn to live with pain. Now you and I are going to go out there and turn a couple of tricks—or you're really going to be talking about pain!"

"Michelle, I can't do it!" I screamed. "I couldn't stand the pain!"

Her face softened. "Okay, okay, I know. Here, let me

get you something." In a moment she came back with a couple of pills—painkillers.

I popped a couple of them and began to feel a tingle. Maybe if I took enough of them, I'd be so high that I wouldn't care what happened.

"Listen, Michelle, please give me about four more of those pills for later on. Okay? They won't last long. When they wear off, I'll just pop a couple more of them, and I won't have to come back here to the apartment and waste time. They really work. Already they're helping me." Without a word she went back into her bedroom and emerged with four more pills.

As we walked out into the hallway, I stopped. "Oops. I guess I'd better go to the bathroom before I hit the street."

"Well, hurry up! I'll wait."

I went back inside and popped those four pills. In a few minutes we hit the street. I could feel the pills taking effect. As I stood on the corner, I kept nodding back and forth, studying the sidewalk carefully.

"Hey, Lori, how many tricks have you had so far?"

That voice! I knew it from somewhere! I turned my blurry eyes in its direction. Lawrence!

"Come on, kid. I asked how many tricks you've had so far."

He sort of drifted in and out of focus. Suddenly I saw him as representing everything that was evil in my life. I wanted out and decided to tell him so.

"Okay, Lawrence, you just get into your car and drive on down the street. I don't want you bugging me anymore. And don't you dare lay a hand on me! I'm through. Do you hear me? Through! T-h-r...."

He grabbed my face between his hands and looked into my eyes searchingly. "Lori, you're high! What have you been taking?"

"What do you mean, high? I said for you to get out of

here before I tear you limb from limb."

I reached back for my switchblade. No bluffing, just as Michelle had told me. This would be for real!

There was nothing there! Then came that vague recollection of hearing it splash in the river the night before.

But Lawrence didn't know I had lost it. He took a swing. I jerked away, and he missed! I raised my hand to hit him, but he just circled around and grabbed me off my feet. Then darkness. . . .

When I came to, I was back in my bed with Lawrence standing over me. I rolled over and buried my head in the pillow. He jerked me back to face him. "Listen, Lori, we have got to have an understanding. I don't know where you got whatever you've been taking, but whatever it is, you're not to take it anymore. Do you understand me?"

I didn't answer. He grabbed my chin and dug his fingernails into my cheek. "When I say something to you, I expect an answer. Now do you understand what I'm talking about?"

I still stared at him blankly.

"All right, kid, if you want to play games, I'll play some, too. For your information, I happened to see Amos on the street. He's still walking around out there. In fact, I worked a deal with him."

That brought me around! "How come he's still walking around? You said you would kill that animal! Do you call that taking care of me?" I slumped back into the pillow.

"I'm taking care of you. Amos and I have a little understanding. He knows he's never to touch you again. He told me he didn't know you were one of my girls. I told him that if he tries anything else, that will be the end of him.

"But, Lori," and he paused ominously. "If you don't

cooperate with me, I'll turn you over to Amos. And you know what Amos will do with you? He'll take you to an apartment and tie your hands and feet to the bed—spread-eagle fashion. And then it's going to be like a circus. Guys are going to come in and pay a good price for his caged tiger!"

"Oh, come on, Lawrence! Nobody'd do a thing like that!"

"Oh, yeah? Fifty percent of those men out on the street are perverts. All I'd have to do would be to take a picture of you in that position, and I could get a hundred bucks apiece! Those bums are looking for a new thrill. I could get fifty guys a day for you that way. And if you think you're hurting now, wait till you get through one of *those* days!"

Lawrence didn't have to try to scare me about perversion. One of the girls on the street told me about the time someone strapped her to a bed and started to pull out the hair from all over her body! She was finally able to escape, but it was one of the most painful experiences of her life.

Another girl told me she had once been kidnapped and taken to the woods and staked out spread-eagle. For two days she lay that way, and the guy kept coming back to her. But she finally escaped.

I didn't want anything to do with these perverts. No telling what these crazies might do. And, knowing Lawrence, he might not stop at anything, especially if he thought I needed to be taught a lesson.

"Okay, you win this time. I'll go back on the street—and I'll stay away from the pills."

"That's better, Lori. And now for the good news. I really had come up to you on the street to tell you about a deal I just made. It means you won't have to go back on the street for a few days. I have a thousand bucks riding on this deal, so whatever you do, kid, don't blow it!"

"A thousand dollars? Who would pay that kind of money?"

"Well, it's a different kind of a deal. There's this businessman I met this morning. He is looking for a girl to go out with his nephew. I understand, from what he says, that the nephew is a brilliant, handsome guy. He's got a master's degree in business administration. This businessman wants to train his nephew to take over his business."

"So what's that got to do with me? I didn't even finish high school. I don't know anything about business."

"Just hang on a minute, Lori, and I'll tell you where you fit in. This businessman lives in Ridgefield, Connecticut, all by himself. He's divorced."

"Uh-huh! I get it. The guy needs a woman, and you're going to use me. No problem."

"Lori, will you stop jumping to conclusions? Wait till I finish!"

"Sorry."

"Well, anyway, this guy wants to have a girl spend a weekend at his place in Connecticut. You see, his nephew is here visiting, and is driving the guy up the wall. All he can talk about is religion. So the businessman wants a sharp chick to come for the weekend.

"And, Lori, I want you to try every trick in the book to get that nephew into bed with you. The man feels that if some chick can get the nephew into bed, he'll have to give up this religious nonsense. Then he can get on with training his nephew to take over his business."

"You mean I'm supposed to stay at this businessman's house, but the businessman doesn't want me; he wants

me to get his handsome nephew into bed. Is that what
you're saying?"

"That's it, exactly! Now, of course, if the businessman wants a little fun, go ahead. But charge him extra
for that. That wasn't part of the deal.

"And here's even more of a challenge. That thousand
bucks is just for you to spend the weekend out there. If
you succeed, he'll up his fee to five thousand dollars!"

"Five thousand dollars? Wow!" I couldn't believe
that much money for one easy weekend.

"Now, Lori, you're the one who came to my mind
when the guy talked to me, but I talked to him before
you got all messed up. So here's what I'll do. He doesn't
want you until the weekend. So you hang around the
apartment and get yourself in shape. By then those
bruises should be gone. At least you'll be feeling a lot
better. Maybe you ought to buy yourself some new
casual clothes—something sexy, you know.

"But whatever you do, don't get high again, or I'll
knock you silly and turn you over to Amos! Do you
understand?"

He didn't have to ask me twice. I sure didn't want to
blow this one. And besides, I'd give almost anything for
a few days rest from the street. And to top it off, a
weekend in Connecticut—probably at a lush estate! If
the guy could afford five thousand dollars for my
services, he was probably filthy rich!

"One thing, Lawrence. What about this nephew? I
mean, what reason should I give for being there for the
weekend? I can't tell him I'm a girl from the street or
anything, can I?"

"Oh, don't be so stupid! Of course you shouldn't tell
him anything like that. You're supposed to be one of this
businessman's secretaries from his business in Manhattan. He's invited you out for the weekend. So you just

pretend you're a secretary. That's no problem, is it?"

"I hope the nephew doesn't ask me to take some dictation or to type. I don't know anything about that."

"Who said secretaries need to know how to type?" He poked at me playfully. "Listen, Lori, you're good at making up stories. So whatever the nephew asks, lie. You can lie well."

Lawrence was right. I knew how to lie. But the thing that was bothering me was this kid's religion. I'd never had any experience with religious nuts.

The week flew by all too quickly as I experimented in making myself as alluring as possible. Friday afternoon I packed an overnight case, and Lawrence took me down on the street to wait for the businessman, George Witmore.

At about six o'clock he drove up in a new Lincoln. He had "success" written all over him. Lawrence introduced us. He seemed like a pleasant, outgoing fellow—and a bit of a rogue.

As we headed for Connecticut, I plied him with questions about the deal. He seemed to be on the level. Frankly, that surprised me. I figured he had some other angle. The whole idea seemed sort of stupid—as though he had to have something to blackmail his own nephew with.

"Are you sure you can handle my nephew?" He eyed me. "I mean, he's a real religious nut. They used to call them 'Jesus freaks.' He says he's not a freak; he's an evangelical, whatever that is."

"Listen, Mr. Witmore, I've had all kinds. There isn't one I can't handle. There's only one thing I'm sorry about."

"What's that?"

"It's the terrible fee you'll have to pay. Five thousand dollars? This is going to be easy!"

He laughed. "Money is no problem for me. That crazy nephew is my problem. It's bad enough he's religious, but now he's trying to convert me! He keeps talking about Jesus coming into a person's heart and living through him. I've never heard anything that strange in all my life—really strange."

We talked easily about a lot of things until we finally came into Ridgefield. It was a beautiful place. And the homes—were they ever expensive!

I couldn't get over his place. I'd seen pictures of places such as this, but had never been to one before.

Something else caught my eye. As we drove up into the driveway, a handsome young man bounded out of the house.

"Uncle, I thought you'd never get here. I'm starved. Oh, who is this ray of sunshine?"

He likes me! I thought. *Maybe this won't be too bad!*

Mr. Witmore introduced me to Rich Witmore. His eyes met mine, and I felt like a star-struck thirteen-year-old again. Wow! Talk about a gorgeous man! I would do this one for nothing!

Mr. Witmore told Rich I was one of his secretaries who was out for the weekend. He didn't seem surprised.

We sat in the living room while the servants put the finishing touches on dinner. I really tried to keep from staring at Rich, but I just couldn't keep my eyes off that man. All the charm I ever had or hoped to have was going to go into this contest—and this handsome young man was going to fall at Lori Hutton's feet!

TEN

That evening the three of us enjoyed a beautiful dinner together by candlelight. We had food that I had only read or heard about before. Both Rich and Mr. Witmore were easy to talk to, and the soft music made it so romantic.

Of course, Mr. Witmore had to tell me all about his estate. He was so proud of it—a twenty-room house, swimming pool, tennis courts, landscaped gardens, and acres of grass and woods. He had a couple of maids, a butler, a gardener, and a chauffeur. I guess this was what I thought Lawrence was like when Michelle first told me about him. Mr. Witmore obviously was extremely wealthy, and Rich was a delight to be around. It was too bad I had to meet up with a pimp like Lawrence before I met these two.

Mr. Witmore casually mentioned his business of building large buildings. I got the hint. I was supposed to know about his business. And he talked about his life in the five years since his divorce had become final. I figured I was supposed to know about that, too, so I didn't ask any questions, but just sort of sympathized with him.

But I did ask Rich questions about himself. And true

to what I expected, he injected religion into the conversation every chance he got. I remember his saying something about "receiving Christ as Saviour." I didn't understand that. From what he said, I guessed that Jesus and Christ were the same. I'd always heard people use those names together when they were cursing. Me? I never really needed religion. But it seemed to make Rich happy.

After dinner we wandered around that absolutely gorgeous home. I laughingly said that a person could get lost without a guide. Mr. Witmore picked up on that one quickly. "Rich will show you anywhere you need to go," he offered.

He had saved the TV room till last. His TV was one of those with a six-foot screen. The three of us settled on a sofa in front of it with me in the middle. We watched for a few minutes. Then, during a commercial, Mr. Witmore mumbled something about a business call he had to make and excused himself, carefully shutting the door behind him. That must be my signal!

I eased over next to Rich. He was already absorbed in the program, but I noticed that he smiled. Maybe this was going to be easier than I had thought!

I gently took his hand. His fingers were so long, like those of an artist or a piano player. Yet he was rugged and every inch a man. I began to rub his hand gently, teasing my fingers over his. He placed his other hand on mine and squeezed lightly.

I snuggled a little closer, and the next thing I knew he put his arm around me and hugged me close. Oh, how wonderful it felt to be in a man's arms this way— especially a gorgeous guy like Rich. A prostitute doesn't have time to love anyone. It was just a business—a disgusting business. But somehow this seemed different. He acted as if he really cared about me.

But Rich's attention quickly shifted back to the TV. After all, it's hard to ignore a six-foot screen! What should I do now?

I decided just to wait and see what developed. I guess we must have sat close like that for half an hour, his arm around me. Every once in a while he'd give me a little hug. And while he was engrossed in the program, I sat there wondering about the whole situation. Was it right to try to seduce such an upstanding young man? He seemed to have so many things going for him. If he could just grow up and forget all this religion nonsense.

Just then someone knocked lightly on the door. Rich pulled his arm away. I turned to see Mr. Witmore open the door a crack. "Lori, could I see you a minute?" he called.

He certainly didn't think I was through already, did he? This was going to take a little time, but I did have Rich on the right track.

He beckoned me out into the hall and then into the living room. "How's it going?" he asked excitedly.

"Well, let's just say the fish is nibbling at the bait!"

"Good! Good! And I just thought of an idea to make this even more interesting. If you seduce Rich tonight, I'll pay ten thousand dollars! I promised Lawrence five thousand dollars if you got to my nephew. But if you can get away with it tonight, I'll add an extra five thousand dollars for you personally. I won't tell Lawrence a thing about it. So that's five thousand bucks for you—extra. What do you think of that?"

"Wow! Five thousand just to make out with your nephew? I can't believe it!"

"Listen, Lori, I've got great plans for that nephew of mine, but they just won't work if he's a religious nut. Rather than building office buildings, he'd probably want to build churches or something; and let me tell you, there's no money in that. So if you get to him, Lori, that extra five thousand dollars is just a drop in the bucket compared to what I'm getting."

"Well, Mr. Witmore, let me tell you something. I have a feeling this is going to be easier than you seem to think. I've got him all set up. Why don't you come back in there with me and tell Rich you'll be gone for a couple of hours and that we have the house to ourselves. It'll all be over before you get back!"

"Good girl, Lori! I guess I picked the right one!"

As we walked back into the TV room, I couldn't believe what I saw. Rich was on his knees! When he heard us, he quickly jumped up.

"What on earth were you doing down there on your knees?" Mr. Witmore demanded. "Did you lose something?"

"Oh, no. I just felt like talking to the Lord—just a little personal problem I needed to discuss with Him. He seemed to understand."

This guy really was a little weird! He acted as though God was right there in the room!

Mr. Witmore said something about being gone for a couple of hours. "Now, Rich," he added, "I want you to see that this little girl enjoys herself! Okay?" He winked at me, and with that, he was gone.

We sat together on the sofa again, and Rich quickly became involved in the program. I reached over and put my hand on his leg, rubbing gently. Without taking his eyes off the screen he took my hand and casually moved it away.

I snuggled up to him and put my head on his chest. "Rich," I whispered, "put your arm around me again; that felt so good."

He drew away. "Lori, I had no right to make those passes at you a few minutes ago. I hardly even know you, and it was wrong of me to put my arm around you the way I did. You are really an attractive girl, and I guess my heart was fluttering a bit too fast. I thought, well, you know, I thought that since we were here together, we could watch TV and maybe get a bit closer. Do you know what I mean?"

So Rich was a red-blooded, all-American boy. His passions had been stirred! Great!

"Come on, Rich; I know how you feel. I guess I probably shouldn't tell you this, but you're the kind of guy I've always dreamed about. I've worked hard as a secretary for your uncle. I could hardly believe it when he invited me out here for the weekend. I hope you don't feel he's pushing me on you...."

I stood up as if to leave. Rich grabbed my arm and pulled me back onto the sofa.

"Well, I don't know what your uncle has in mind. But you don't need to be afraid of me, Rich. I assure you that nothing will happen that you or I will be ashamed of. I'm not that kind of girl. So why don't we just sit here and hold hands, okay?"

Silence. He just stared at the screen—almost as if he was afraid to even look at me.

Finally he said, "If it's okay with you, Lori, let's not even hold hands. You know how one thing can lead to another." Strike two!

Somehow I had to get this young man back on the track again. The direct, frontal attack wasn't going to work. It would have to be something more subtle. But I had only two hours!

Just then a John Wayne movie came on. "Yippee!" Rich shouted. "John Wayne is my favorite actor! What could be better than sitting here with you watching a John Wayne movie! This has got to be my lucky day!"

By the look on Rich's face I knew he was a great deal

more excited about watching John Wayne than sitting next to me! I knew I was in trouble, and I could see five thousand dollars sailing out the window. No woman on earth could get Rich's attention now.

Two hours later when Mr. Witmore returned, he walked right into the TV room. One glance at the TV told him nothing had happened. Rich hardly even looked up to acknowledge his uncle's presence.

Mr. Witmore motioned me out of the room again. As I got up, I patted Rich's cheek. He smiled and turned quickly back to the TV. John Wayne was about to get the Indians.

"Well, Lori, you don't need to tell me," Mr. Witmore began. "Rich has more of a passion for Westerns than he does for women. Nothing happened. Right?"

"Right. It's just too bad I didn't bring a cowgirl outfit. Maybe then I could have gotten his attention."

He laughed. "Well, let's not give up yet. I'll tell you what I did while I was out. I've made arrangements for you and Rich to go to Studio Fifty-four tomorrow evening. The owner is a personal friend of mine, and he'll be expecting you. They have a fantastic disco there, and everything will be on me. How about that?"

"Do you mean Studio Fifty-four on Fifty-fourth Street? Wow! I've heard that place is absolutely fantastic! A lot of movie stars go there."

"Right! I've met a few of them when I've been there. You just tell the owner who you are, and he'll give you the red-carpet treatment. In fact, if there are any movie stars there tomorrow night, he said he'd personally introduce you to them. I know it will be a fantastic evening for you, and maybe Rich will get turned on. I'm sure you've got the charms to do it!"

"Yes! I'll give him a dance he'll never forget!"

"Good! Now one more thing. When you and Rich get back here, I'll make sure I'm in bed. So if you can, when you walk in that front door, lead him right up to your bedroom.

"By the way, if you can get him to take a drink or two, that might help, too. So help me, I've got liquor in every corner of this house. Never once has he touched it. I guess the guy doesn't drink. And I've never heard him swear. Would you believe he doesn't even drink milk?"

We both laughed at that one. This Rich was really straight! I couldn't help but admire him for having convictions. But then, I was here on business.

"I've made arrangements for my chauffeur to drive you tomorrow. That way you and Rich can be together in the backseat and do whatever you want to do. Do you read me?"

I knew. But that was tomorrow night! Had he already given up on tonight? I didn't want to lose the extra bonus, so I asked him about it.

"Hey, no problem. I know Rich is a tough one, so let's just say the extra five thousand dollars still stands for the whole weekend."

I started back toward the TV room, but Rich had flipped off the set and was on his way out. "Fantastic movie, Uncle George," he said. "That John Wayne is some actor! He always comes through."

"What did you think of it, Lori?" Mr. Witmore asked.

"It was too bad he had to watch that old movie," I answered. "I prefer wrestling." And I slyly winked at him.

"Huh? No kidding?" Rich said, looking stunned. "Do you really like to watch wrestling?"

"No, Rich. I was just pulling your leg. My favorite thing is really disco dancing! I mean, I really love that. How about you?"

"No, not really," Rich replied. "I like watching Westerns, playing tennis, reading my Bible, and going to church—and not necessarily in that order."

Mr. Witmore laughed. "Oh, come on, Rich, you've got to start enjoying life a little. Western movies and tennis may be okay, but the church and Bible bit is for old ladies—or for people getting ready to die.

"Now listen to this, nephew. I think you may have disappointed Lori by getting so involved in that TV movie tonight. So here's what I'm going to do so you can redeem yourself. Since Lori loves disco dancing, I've made arrangements for the two of you to go to Studio Fifty-four tomorrow evening. Everything will be on me. You two will have a fantastic evening. I know you will!"

I glanced at Rich. He was busy studying his feet.

"What do you think about that, Lori?" Mr. Witmore asked. "Do you want to go to Studio Fifty-four?"

"Oh, wow! Mr. Witmore. I've always wanted to go to Studio Fifty-four. That would be absolutely fantastic! And to have Rich as my escort—what girl could ask for more? That is, if Rich really wants to take me. . . ."

"Oh, I want to take you, Lori. It's just that . . . well, I'd better think that one over."

He turned and started to walk away. I could tell he was embarrassed. Was disco dancing against his religion?

"I guess I'll turn in for the night, if it's okay with you two. It's been a long day."

"Sure, Rich," his uncle answered. "Sleep well, because you're going to get a lot of exercise tomorrow evening!"

"Oh, speaking of exercise," Rich said as he turned to face us again, "Lori, why don't we play a couple of sets of tennis in the morning?"

"Tennis? I've never even held a tennis racket."

"No problem," Mr. Witmore said. "Rich is a great teacher."

"Yes," Rich answered. "I love to teach pretty girls

how to play—tennis, that is!" Then with a good night to both of us, he was gone.

"Hey, Lori, this is a good turn of luck," Mr. Witmore said. "First thing in the morning I'll run down to the sport shop and get you a tennis outfit. I mean, I'll bet you look like a dream in white. What size do you take?"

"Well, I'm a size seven. Will I need shoes? I wear six-A."

"Great, just great! And besides buying you a tennis outfit, I'll pick you up a disco dress. It'll be a real disco dress!"

I knew what he had in mind—a sexy tennis outfit and a sexy disco dress. Poor Rich. How was he going to handle this? I had a beautiful body—I knew that. And Mr. Witmore wanted to be sure it was displayed to the best advantage!

Mr. Witmore told me he usually had breakfast at nine o'clock and that Rich often joined him. He said I could have my breakfast in bed if I wanted it. I thanked him and said I thought it would be best if I joined them at breakfast.

Well, I could hardly sleep that night. I don't really know what kept me awake. Was it all this wealth? I certainly wasn't accustomed to such luxury. Or was it Rich? He seemed to be such an outstanding young man, one with high moral standards. Was it right of me to try to seduce him?

I rolled and tossed most of the night, trying to come up with answers. But when morning came, I was no closer to a solution than before. After all, I was supposed to be here on business. If it weren't for that proposition, I wouldn't be here at all. I'd better swallow any noble thoughts and give the job my best!

I got up and showered in the luxury of a private bath just off my room. And those towels—I could almost sink away in them!

Right at nine o'clock I went down to breakfast. Rich
and Mr. Witmore were waiting for me.

Talk about a fantastic breakfast: eggs, sausage,
cereal, juice, toast, biscuits, gravy, potatoes, and all
kinds of fresh fruit. I've never seen a spread like it—and
so tasty. I know I ate too much.

"Rich, I went down and got a tennis outfit for Lori
this morning," Mr. Witmore announced. Then he
proudly displayed it. The shorts were slit up the side,
exposing the upper part of my thigh. I was right. Mr.
Witmore wanted me to expose some flesh. Would Rich
be able to concentrate on his game? Men can be so
naive!

Then he showed us the dress. As I expected, it was
very low-cut. When I got in it, Rich's eyes would bug
out!

I changed in ten minutes flat and hurried down to the
tennis court. Rich was hitting the ball around, waiting.
He gave a low whistle when he saw me.

Very gently he taught me the basics of the game. I
especially liked the part where he taught me how to
hold the racket. He got right up behind me and put his
arms around me. It felt so tender, as though my Prince
Charming were about to sweep me off my feet. Was I
the one who was getting carried away with impossible
dreams?

We spent a couple of hours hitting the ball back and
forth. I really couldn't call it tennis, and he gallantly
didn't keep score. But I was getting the hang of it, and
Rich at least acted as though he enjoyed it.

The maid served our lunch by the pool. Mr. Witmore
made himself scarce, stopping by only long enough to
announce that he had picked up a swimsuit for me, too.
Then he pulled out of his pocket the briefest little bikini
I had ever seen.

We swam later that afternoon. I just kept watching

Rich. I don't think he ever really looked at me. In fact, he seemed a bit defensive. Never mind! Wait until this evening. He would be in for a big surprise!

That evening when I came down in my disco dress, I met Rich in the living room. He looked sharp in a suit. This time when I entered the room, he looked me over and declared, "Lori, you are really beautiful!"

"Thanks," I said. And I knew I had him. His eyes looked up and down my body. This was going to be the night!

We walked out the front door to where the chauffeur was waiting for us. I noticed that Rich was carrying a book with a black cover. Strange.

As we settled into the backseat of the Lincoln, Rich kept the black book on his lap. I couldn't help but stare at it. Finally my curiosity got the best of me. "Rich, what's that black book?"

"Black book? Oh, that's my Bible."

"Bible?" I returned, not really believing what I was hearing. "What on earth are you doing with the Bible tonight?"

"The Bible is the greatest Book in the world, Lori. It tells us how to live. It teaches us the principles of life. When you really do what it says, you can't imagine the joy and peace you'll have."

Uh-oh! Now I was going to get the sermon! Was this Rich's way of getting out of taking me to Studio Fifty-four? I pushed away from him and stared out of the window. Rich sensed my coolness and dropped the subject.

Then something hit me, and I wheeled toward him. "Rich, you're not planning to take that Bible into the disco and read it while we're trying to dance, are you?"

"Oh, no!" he laughed. "I wouldn't do something like that. There's a place for everything."

I was soon to find out what he meant by that!

ELEVEN

We were soon traveling along the Merritt Parkway. Rich didn't say much, and that Bible of his kept bugging me. He had said he wasn't going to read it while we danced. Then a wild thought hit me. What if he went into Studio 54 and made like a preacher! How embarrassing!

But before I had a chance to ask him about that possibility, the car slowed, and we exited from the parkway. I knew this wasn't the way to mid-Manhattan. "Hey! How come we're turning off here?"

"Oh, I just asked the chauffeur to take a little detour."

He wasn't planning on taking me out on some deserted country road, was he? Certainly not with the chauffeur along!

By this time we were driving through a small town. "Turn here," Rich said. Then about half a block farther he told the driver to pull up in front of a building. Then I saw the sign: COMMUNITY BIBLE CHURCH.

"Okay, Rich, what in the world are we doing at a church?"

"Come on, Lori. We're going to start our evening by

going in here and hearing some fantastic things. I know you're going to like it. I sure do!"

"You have to be kidding!" I screamed. "I haven't been in a church since I went to help someone with a Sunday-school contest. I think I was seven! Church has nothing to offer me."

Rich laughed. "You sound just like I used to sound. I thought I was too intellectual and, frankly, too good for church. Church might be okay for old ladies and little kids, but it had nothing to offer a man-of-the-world college man like me. But then I found out something different."

"But, Rich, this is Saturday night. People don't go to church on Saturday night, do they?"

"Oh, this is a special Saturday night. They're having a girls' choir from the Walter Hoving Home to sing at a youth rally. I know you'll enjoy these girls."

"A what from where?"

"A choir from the Walter Hoving Home. That's the Teen Challenge girls home up in Garrison, New York. All of these girls used to be addicts, alcoholics, and delinquents. They have been born again through Jesus' love. Some of them have formed a choir, and they're here to sing tonight. And some of them will be telling how Jesus changed their lives."

I stared at Rich. Did he suspect who I really was and what I was up to? I hoped his uncle hadn't spilled the beans by trying to weasel out of that deal with Lawrence. No, that didn't make sense. If Mr. Witmore was really trying to get me into bed with Rich, he certainly wouldn't have told Rich about our scheme. But maybe this wasn't the first time Uncle George had pulled a caper such as this on Rich. I had to find out if Rich knew what was going on. Had he accidentally stumbled onto it?

"You say these girls were addicts and alcoholics. Do you know if any of them were prostitutes?"

He looked startled. I held my breath. Maybe he was too embarrassed to say.

"Listen, Lori, these girls have been into all kinds of things. Yes, I know some of them have been into prostitution, but I want to tell you something. It really doesn't matter what kind of sin we have been in, because Jesus still loves us. You may be a nice, sweet, innocent secretary working for my uncle, but I can tell there's something down deep within your heart that's crying out for reality—and that reality is Jesus."

I took a deep breath. He didn't know! But he was right about that longing to know a real life. He didn't know how right he was. Oh, how I wished I could find something worth living for.

"Rich," I said, making my voice sound as hurt as I could, "I really think you tricked me. I'm dressed for disco, not for church. But I'll make a deal with you. Studio Fifty-four will be open late. I'll go to church with you, if you'll take me to the disco afterward."

"Lori, you're supposed to be my guest tonight. A little church meeting won't hurt you. And I will make the deal with you. If you go to church with me and afterward you still want to go down to Studio Fifty-four, we'll go down there. You can do all the discoing you want. I don't dance, but I'll find some people to talk to. I'm sure I can find somebody there I can tell about the thrill of knowing the Lord. So you can do the discoing, and I'll do the sharing. Okay?"

That really wasn't the kind of evening I had had in mind. But I could tell that getting him to Studio 54 wouldn't work out the way Mr. Witmore had planned, anyway. Sure, I'd much rather go discoing than to be in this little church out here in the dingleberries. But I knew I really didn't have much choice in the matter.

"Okay, Rich Witmore, you've outfoxed me this time. We'll go to church first. Then we'll go down to Studio Fifty-four. I'll do my dancing, and you can do your preaching. I'm sure you'll find more lost souls down there than you will here!"

"Lori, you're all right!" He patted my arm. "I really like you because you're such a good sport. Come on, let's go inside."

People were standing around outside waiting for the service to begin. Most of them recognized Rich. You would have thought it was Old Home Week. He threw his arms around them and gave them big hugs. This group certainly was friendly.

Of course, he introduced me to some of his friends. They all seemed likable enough. These Christian young men weren't sissies, either. A couple of them had football sweaters on. Rich explained to me that they were using their athletic abilities for the glory of the Lord—whatever that meant. He said that being a Christian and a good football player worked hand in hand. I didn't quite follow that since I didn't know much about football—or Christians.

Once inside, I started toward the back row, but Rich grabbed my arm and guided me right up to the front! What rotten luck. I figured if I was in the back, I could sneak out if I got too bored. But now Rich had me. He probably did it on purpose.

The meeting began with singing. I must say, I've never heard singing like that before. Talk about enthusiasm! Everybody clapped their hands and really seemed to enjoy their religion. Every once in a while someone would shout out, "Amen!" or, "Praise the

Lord!" It wasn't like anything I had imagined about church, but it was exciting, and all the people seemed so happy.

When the choir from the Walter Hoving Home started to sing, something about their music really got to me. One of the girls would introduce each song by telling about her past life. I could see by her radiant face that something really had happened to her.

As they sang, one of the girls kept glancing right at me and smiling. Her smile was so contagious that I smiled back, without really thinking about it. I almost said I noticed her because she stood out from the rest. That really wasn't true. She was in a wheelchair.

In a whisper I asked Rich about her. He said he didn't know, but probably she had had a problem with drugs.

I couldn't get over her beautiful smile. How could someone who had to stay in a wheelchair smile that way?

One of the girls introduced herself as Sherry Banister and began to tell us about her past life.

"I can remember one night when I was tripping on drugs," she started. "I was lying on the floor of my parents' living room, and it came over me that I just had to die. So I went into the kitchen, got a butcher knife, returned to the living room, and proceeded to cut my arms up. Blood ran all over the place. My mother ran into the living room and started screaming. She called an ambulance, and I was rushed to the hospital and sewed up. Then I was sent away to a mental institution."

Unconsciously I edged forward in my seat. This girl had the same kind of problems I had. I wondered how she had overcome hers.

"People thought I was crazy," she continued. "I don't know if you can believe this or not, but I had twenty shock treatments. I knew I wasn't crazy, but since I had

tried to kill myself, the people at the hospital felt that
shock treatments would cure me. But no matter what
they did to me, I knew that someday I would succeed in
killing myself. It was just a matter of time."

My mind drifted to the many times I'd tried suicide.
Why hadn't I succeeded? Was there some power—
maybe God—who really spared my life? Or was it just
luck? Would my life still end tragically? Maybe
someone would murder me!

"After I was released from the mental institution,"
she went on, "I did stay off drugs for a time. But still
there was that emptiness in my heart that nothing
seemed to fill. My parents rejected me because they
thought I was crazy. I couldn't convince them that I
wasn't.

"Anyway, one evening I decided that life just wasn't
worth living. I bought some pills and ended up taking
one hundred hits of amphetamines and about ten hits of
acid."

I gritted my teeth. No one could take that much and
make it!

"I just totally flipped out. I don't think I came to for
several days. When I came around, I didn't know where
I was. I simply found myself lying in some woods. It
had been raining, and I was soaking wet, with mud all
over me. I thought I had been dreaming and that I was
floating above my body and was just hearing pretty
music and feeling so peaceful. But then I woke up and
realized I was right back where I had come from.

"Slowly I pulled myself out of that mud and looked.
My clothes were half-torn off me. Probably I had been
raped! My undergarments were missing.

"Friends, I cannot stand here and tell you how I felt. I
felt like a dirty, filthy animal. Who had taken me when I
was out of my mind and brought me to those woods, I'll

never know. But one thing I did know: I had to die. My folks thought I was crazy; the doctors thought I was crazy. I had absolutely no hope whatsoever, and I felt lower than anyone could get.

"I staggered out of the woods and flagged down a car. The driver slowed down, but when he saw what I looked like, he took off. I stood there, cursing.

"I waited for another car. Same thing. I guess, looking back, I really can't blame them. I must have looked like something from hell. But finally a car stopped.

"Can you believe who those people were? They were Christians!"

I knew I was getting to the sermon part of her story, but I didn't care. I really wanted to know what had changed her.

"The Christians took me to their home. They told me to take a shower, and they gave me some clean clothes. I couldn't get over how lovingly they treated me. I must admit I thought I had died or was dreaming. How could anyone be so nice to someone like me? They didn't know me. I couldn't do anything for them.

"But one thing I learned right from the beginning— they didn't think I was crazy. In fact, they held out a great hope for my future. Of course, I didn't understand it then the way I do now, but they said that God had a plan for my life, and that that plan was a plan for good. It sounded weird, but the shower and the clean clothes weren't.

"They fixed a lovely dinner for me and afterward told me about Jesus. What they said seemed too good to be true. They said He wanted to forgive me for all my sins and give me peace, that He wanted to give me a reason for living. They described it as 'putting a song within my heart and a skip to my step.' I thought that was beautiful."

This seemed so unreal. Just a little while ago I thought I was headed toward Studio 54 and an evening of disco. Now I was sitting in church, and a girl was telling me about something that I didn't even know existed!

Sherry went on, "In the living room of the people's home they explained to me how to receive Jesus as my personal Saviour. All I had to do, they said, was to ask Him to forgive my sins and open my heart to Him. Then He would come in and make me a new person.

"In a very simple way I prayed, asking Jesus to forgive me. Then I invited Him into my heart. Friends, when I did that, I must confess nothing happened. I still felt like the same person, and I still had some great fears."

Aha! I said to myself. *I knew it. It's too good to be true! It really doesn't work!*

But Sherry went on: "The next day I knew something had happened. I had gone to bed and slept like I have never slept before. I often used to take pills to put me to sleep—but not that night. Without any medication at all I slept like a baby. I didn't awaken until one o'clock in the afternoon. When I got up, that's when it happened: The birds sang in my heart, and the sun burst forth from behind the clouds. I *knew* I was saved. Jesus had changed my life, just as He said He would. He had given me a peace that is impossible to describe. All the bitterness and anger were washed out of my life. I stood there, completely clean, through the blood of Jesus!"

I had become so engrossed that I felt a tear trickle down my cheek. I reached in my purse for a handkerchief.

More tears flowed. I glanced at Rich, hoping he wouldn't notice. He was crying, too. Why? When he saw the tears in my eyes, he smiled and put his arm around me.

He gave me just a little hug—a different kind of hug. There was no lust in it. It just seemed so pure and holy. And I had to admit to myself that it felt good to be in church!

Sherry went on to tell us that she was going to graduate from the Walter Hoving Home in about four weeks and then was going to a Bible school.

When she sat down, everybody clapped and clapped for her. I did, too, as I've never clapped before. I was so happy for her.

Then I sat there, almost stunned. I just couldn't get over what I had heard. Her life sounded so much like mine. If God could do something like that for Sherry, could He—would He—do it for me?

I hated to get my hopes up, but maybe there was something to this religion that Rich kept talking about.

TWELVE

After Sherry's talk I was too deep in thought to remember much else about the service. I kept wondering whether something like this could ever happen to me.

Before I knew it, I heard the pastor saying, "If any of you would like to receive Jesus as your Saviour, please come up here to the front, and I'll be glad to pray with you."

Something inside me urged me to go up there, but I really didn't understand what it was all about, and I was too embarrassed to stand up.

A couple of teenagers did walk up to the front, and he prayed with them. It all seemed so nice. *Is that all there is to receiving Jesus?* I wondered.

After the benediction, Rich and I started toward the door. Every so often he'd stop and hug somebody. Then he asked if I wanted to go up front and meet the girls from the Walter Hoving Home. Oh, no! One of them would probably recognize me as being from the street! So I gave a weak excuse and said I'd wait for him if he wanted to go up there.

I got a little jealous watching him with all of those girls. They seemed to be so enthusiastic about meeting him. And it also gave me time to see him in a new light. He had virtues I wished I had—like such a positive outlook on life. He seemed to know where he was going. Still, for ten thousand dollars I had to convince him that my body was worth more than what he had. I got this feeling that maybe this wasn't going to work after all—and I was almost glad!

Then I noticed that girl in the wheelchair pushing her way down the aisle toward me—still smiling. I turned away for just a minute, and there she was, right beside me. "Did you enjoy the service tonight?"

"I sure did!" I answered. "Especially that girl who talked. She was absolutely fantastic. By the time she got through, I was crying!" Just thinking about it must have overwhelmed me because the tears started flowing again.

She reached up and took my arm gently. "I've never met you before," she said, "and I really don't know who you are or why you came tonight. But all during the service, God's Spirit kept drawing me to you. God has told me you have been deeply hurt and disillusioned with life, and when I came down here, I knew that was right. I saw your wrists."

I glanced down. It hadn't been that long since the prison episode. Would I ever be able to hide my scars? How embarrassing!

"Yes, you're right. Some of the things Sherry talked about I've been through, too."

"Could I tell you a little about my experience?" she asked. "God has been so good to me. If you've got just a minute, I'd like to tell you about it."

What could I say? Rich was still talking, and this girl looked so kind.

"Sure! I'd love to hear what's happened to you."

She nudged her wheelchair over to where no one was standing and motioned for me to follow. "Why don't you sit down here," she suggested, "so we can talk eyeball to eyeball."

As I sat down, she said, "My name's Debbie Wallingberg. What's yours?"

"Lori Hutton."

"Well, Lori, my story is like Sherry's. I was on drugs for a number of years. One time I got high and climbed a tree. I thought I was a bird. Thinking I could fly, I jumped. I landed on my back, and was rushed to a hospital. Doctors did everything, but nothing helped. Lori, I'll never walk again."

"Oh, I'm so sorry!" I gasped. "But you seem to be so brave about it all. How come?"

"Well, I wasn't always. When I first learned the truth, I tried to kill myself. See these wrists?" She held out her hands. Like mine, they were scarred.

"I know what it's all about," she went on. "I guess we both know what it's like to feel so hopeless and empty. We do have one thing in common, don't we? We both tried to kill ourselves.

"But in my case, I knew I would never walk again. There was absolutely no hope left for me. I was an athlete in high school. I had too much pride to spend the rest of my life confined to a wheelchair. I didn't want people caring for me. I didn't want people catering to me. So several times I tried to kill myself. Obviously, I never succeeded." She smiled.

"My family tried everything to help me. I've been to I don't know how many psychiatrists to straighten out my head. No way in the world was I about to accept being crippled.

"Then, Lori, a beautiful thing happened. A psychia-

trist told me about the Walter Hoving Home. Because
of my drug problem, they accepted me into their
program. I thought it would be like going to a mental
institution. But when I got to that beautiful place, I
knew something about it was different. In fact, when
we drove onto the property, I could feel something
about that place. It was so peaceful.

"And you can't believe how the girls treated me!
They just couldn't do enough. Then on the second day,
it happened."

"What happened?"

"The second day I received Jesus into my heart. A
miracle took place. I was born again into a new life with
Jesus. And, Lori, when I received Jesus, I was still in my
wheelchair. But I stood up on the inside! And now for
these past months I've been walking hand in hand with
Him. It is beautiful!"

Through her smile tears coursed down her cheeks—
and that started me crying again, too. What this Jesus
gave to these girls baffled me. It sounded so wonderful.
But if only these girls knew who they were talking to—a
prostitute who had tried to kill herself because nobody
wanted her!

"Lori, Jesus wants to do the same for you. I know you
have some real problems, but Jesus wants to change
you right now."

"Yes, I do have problems. All I can say is that my past
is bad, very bad. I believe what's happened to you, but I
can't believe it's for me."

"Oh, Lori, it is! It is! All you have to do is receive
Jesus as your Saviour, and everything will turn out
right!"

Once again my tears started to flow. I glanced up and
saw Rich headed our way. Oh, no! I couldn't let him see

me crying again. He might suspect something about me!

I knew it was rude to leave that crippled girl so abruptly, but I had to get out of there. I half-ran down the front steps. Now where was our car? I spotted it parked about a block away and ran toward it.

Slightly out of breath, I jumped in the backseat. The chauffeur turned around. "My goodness, Lori, you've been crying! Did they hurt you?"

"Oh, no. I guess I'm crying because I'm happy. Those people in there have great hope and peace."

Rich had seen me take off, and he hurried after me. "Lori, are you okay?" I nodded.

"I guess I owe you an apology," he said as he got in. "I really didn't expect this service to be so dynamic. Several times I noticed that you were crying. But I think you enjoyed it, didn't you?"

"Did I enjoy it? This evening was the greatest experience in my life, Rich. I mean, it was absolutely overwhelming. I didn't know that reality like this existed! I thought that Sherry was unbelievable. And, Rich, that crippled girl talked to me. She'll never walk again, but she said that because of Jesus she's standing up on the inside! Now *that* is hard to believe!"

Rich grinned. "Lori, what you've seen and heard tonight *is* the real thing. I visited the Walter Hoving Home a few weeks ago, and what those girls said is true. They have experienced something that the world needs to know. I think it's something you need to know, too."

"Yes, you're on the right path, Rich. I guess a well-adjusted secretary from your uncle's business needs that, too."

"Right, Lori. Everybody does." He patted my hand. "Okay, let's head for Studio Fifty-four. The night is young, and as soon as I hit that door, I'm going to preach a sermon like they've never heard before!"

"Uh, Rich, why don't we just go get a cup of coffee or something. I think I've had enough entertainment for one evening."

His eyes met mine. "Lori, honestly, I was just kidding about the preaching. God wants us to use wisdom. I wouldn't embarrass you. But we made a deal. You can go down there if you want to. I'll just sit and wait. And I'd wait a long time for you!"

"Oh, Rich, you're so sweet. The more I'm around you, the more I like you. Thanks, but I really don't feel like going."

His strong arm drew me close. "And I might say, for a secretary in Uncle George's business, you're one of the nicest girls I've ever met!"

He squeezed me gently. Was I falling in love with him? That would never work out!

The chauffeur drove us to a diner, and Rich invited him to join us for some coffee and dessert. In that relaxed atmosphere Rich told me a little more about himself. He said he wanted to become a businessman and share Christ with other businessmen in New York City. He knew his uncle wanted to train him for his business, but there seemed to be some problem, and his uncle wouldn't tell him what.

If he only knew what his uncle had in mind for him! Somehow I just wasn't up to crawling into bed with Rich for any amount of money!

When we got back to the house, I noticed that all the lights were still burning. Strange!

Rich's uncle was in the living room waiting for us, and next to him stood Honey Simmons. My mouth flew open. When she saw me, she gasped. Honey was

another prostitute I had seen often around Times
Square.

Before I could say anything, Mr. Witmore gave me a
knowing glance. "Lori, this is Raquel Balio. She's a
secretary in one of my businesses in Denver. She's here
for the weekend, looking over some new products with
me."

This uncle was something else. Why did he have
Honey Simmons here? Maybe he thought if I couldn't
get to Rich, Honey could. She was beautiful and
seductive.

I played along. "I'm very happy to know you,
Raquel. I hope your trip to the city is successful."

Mr. Witmore went on, "Raquel, this is my nephew
Rich. I believe I've mentioned him. He's a fantastic
young man who is on the rise in the business world.
Someday he's going to be one of the world's great
businessmen."

Rich blushed at that. I couldn't believe it. I don't
know how long it had been since I'd seen a grown man
blush! What a guy that Rich was.

"Did you two have a great time at Studio Fifty-
four?" Mr. Witmore asked.

"Oh, uncle, you can't imagine the fantastic time we
had tonight," Rich answered. "Didn't we, Lori?"

"Yes, the greatest! I mean, I was absolutely
overwhelmed. I think it will last me forever!"

Mr. Witmore brightened. "Well, Raquel and I have
some business to talk over. We'll be upstairs in my
office. Why don't you two relax and take it easy?" He
winked at me.

No sooner had they left than Rich said, "I think I'll
retire for the evening." I looked into his eyes and could
see ten thousand dollars flying away. Was there no way

I could get to this guy? I had to try, or I'd be in big trouble.

"I know you must be tired, Rich, but why don't we watch TV for a while? Maybe there's another Western on."

"Come on, Lori. You said you didn't like Westerns. Besides, I've already checked the schedule. No Westerns are on."

"Rich, sit down here by me for a minute." Like a child, he obeyed. I snuggled up to him and ran my fingers through his hair. I could feel him relax. He seemed to be enjoying it.

"How about a nice, snappy game of tennis in the morning? I think I need some more lessons." Maybe if he saw me in that tennis outfit now, he'd get some ideas.

"Sounds like fun, but I'm going to church in the morning. Why don't you come with me?" Church again? I didn't think I could stand another service so soon!

"Thanks, but church really isn't my bag, Rich. I'll just swim in the morning till you get back. Besides, what if I went to church and started to bawl again?"

Rich laughed. "Lori, you don't need to be ashamed of tears. Christians sometimes cry when they hurt; they also cry when they're happy. Besides, I think it's good for a person to cry."

"Well, maybe for you, but I don't know about me. I've got to think through what happened tonight."

Rich got up, stretched, and started toward the stairway. "Good night, Lori," he said as he yawned.

At the bottom of the stairway, he turned toward me again. "Lori?"

"Yes, Rich. What is it?"

"Something's kind of bothering me. I hope you don't mind my asking."

"Shoot."

"Well, when we came in tonight, I couldn't help but notice the way you reacted when you saw Raquel. Do you know her?"

Oh, no! Now was the time for what Lawrence had said: "Lie!"

"Rich, I'll level with you. I haven't told you everything about myself. I've had some real disasters in my family. My older sister Bonita died of a drug overdose. When I saw Raquel, it startled me. She looks exactly like Bonita, and all of those memories came rushing back."

"I'm sorry, Lori. I guess I shouldn't have asked."

"It's okay, Rich. I'm too prone to carry my feelings on my sleeve!"

He said good night again and walked up the stairs. I saw no point in sitting there alone in the living room, so I went up to my room and just sat there for a long time, staring out the window. I had to think about what had happened tonight.

Those girls from the Walter Hoving Home—they really had something. But look at me. Look at how easy it was for me to lie to Rich—a good, clean-cut, handsome man whom any girl would give her right arm to have for a husband—and here I was, lying to him, even about a phony sister. If he found out the truth, whatever would he think of me?

I thought people were supposed to sleep better in the country, but I didn't sleep well that night, either. Hour after hour my life paraded before me, and what I saw really upset me. Couldn't I somehow be a better person?

I finally fell into a troubled sleep—and didn't awaken till nearly noon. When I went downstairs, the maid offered me some coffee and asked if I wanted anything else. I really wasn't hungry.

At about one o'clock Rich came home from church. When I saw him pull into the driveway, I rushed upstairs and put on that sexy tennis outfit. Then I bounded down the stairs, looking for him. He was in the library, reading.

"Hey, Rich! Look at this!" I stuck my chest out as far as I could and put my hands on my hips. "You like what you see?"

"Lori, you should give up being a secretary and become a model. You're absolutely gorgeous!"

Aha! Maybe I had him coming my way. First we'd start with tennis lessons. The ten thousand dollars came in sight again.

Then he looked so serious. "Lori, there's something I should have mentioned to you last night. Would you mind if we took a little walk together instead of playing tennis?"

"Why not? I'd kind of like to explore the woods." This would be a better plan than tennis. I'd get him away from the house and....

We walked along the path that led through the woods. Finally we came upon a white bench along the path. "Let's sit here for a minute, Lori. I've got to tell you something I know all about."

What in the world would he want to say to me?

Well, in a moment I found out—and I couldn't believe what he was telling me!

THIRTEEN

"Lori, I don't quite know how to tell you this, but I'm on to your game."

"What?" I asked incredulously. "What did you say, Rich?"

"I said I know why you're really here this weekend."

Certainly Rich had no idea about his uncle's plan to get him into bed with me. I knew I'd better play dumb.

"Well, you might as well just calm down, Rich. If you think I conned your uncle into inviting me up here so I could meet Mr. Wonderful, you're barking up the wrong tree!"

He just stared at me, a kind of hurt look touching the edges of his eyes. I knew I'd better try another angle. "Of course you know why I'm here this weekend—so you could give me a little religion."

"Well, kind of," he answered. "That's very important, Lori, but that's not the reason you came. You're here to try to entice me to have an intimate relationship with you."

I gasped. How could he possibly know?

"Rich, that is absolutely wrong!" I jumped off the

bench to emphasize my shock and dismay. "That is one of the most disgusting things I've ever heard. You think every girl in the world just can't wait to jump into bed with you. Well, mister, you listen to me! Just because you got hot and bothered watching TV the other night doesn't mean I'm easy. I'm as clean as they make them, buster."

Rich's face reddened. "Lori, please! This is difficult enough as it is. Please sit down. I want to tell you more."

I had hoped my show of anger would throw him off the track. But had I convinced him? I stood there defiantly, hands on hips, daring him to accuse me of anything. But he looked so gentle and hurt that it was hard to maintain that pose. So I slowly gave in and sat down—at the far end of the bench.

"Thanks, Lori. Now please don't go flying off again when I tell you the rest of the story. My wonderful uncle not only is an important businessman; he also operates a house of prostitution."

I jumped up again and screamed. "Rich, these accusations are absolutely ridiculous. I've worked for your uncle for three years now. Never once has he touched me or any of the girls in the office. Ninety percent of the girls there would love to crawl into bed with him, but he has stayed absolutely clean. He's a real gentleman!"

"Okay, Lori. But please sit down again. I'm not through."

He was getting too close for comfort. I had to think of something else. But as I stood there staring at him, he took my arm and gently pulled me down beside him. "You know Raquel—the one who came in with my uncle last night?" he asked.

"I suppose you think she's a prostitute, right?"

"Right. I *know* she is."

"For crying out loud, Rich, this is one of the most ridiculous conversations I've ever had. I can't imagine a religious person like you lying like this. What's the matter with you, anyway?"

"I'm not lying, Lori. Please let me go on." I nodded. I might as well find out what he really knew.

"Two weeks ago a girl named Laverne Coller came out here. She's a prostitute from the Times Square area. Anyway, she tried to make advances, but I had a chance to talk to her about Christ. She broke down and cried like a baby. I discovered she had been raised in a wonderful Christian family but had run away from her home in Minneapolis. Lori, I had the beautiful experience of helping her back to Christ. She got out of prostitution, and now she's gone back home to her family."

I just stared at him. How had he figured out what his uncle was up to?

"Furthermore, Lori, Laverne told me all about my uncle and his house of prostitution in Elizabeth, New Jersey. Of course, he *is* a successful businessman in Manhattan. But that's not all.

"He's got two things in mind when he invites girls out here for the weekend. And, by the way, you're not the first one, you know. Anyway, his major purpose is to get me to fall into sin with a girl. Number two is that after he gets you girls out here, he tries to hire you away from your pimps so you'll end up working for him.

"You see, I went down and investigated his house of prostitution last week. It is really a gorgeous place. He's trying to make prostitution a legitimate business. He says there's lots of profit in it, and he doesn't see anything wrong with it. I talked to a couple of girls down there. They said my uncle treats them well, and they keep fifty percent of the earnings. Uncle George has a husband and wife running the place and is very discreet about it. The girls have to have regular physical checkups. It appears very legitimate, but there's one problem. It's illegal!"

I sat there, stunned. So this was why Mr. Witmore had brought me here—to hire me away from Lawrence. If Lawrence had any idea what was going on, he'd kill him! But what should I do now that I knew all of this? Should I admit to Rich that he was right and go to work for Mr. Witmore? It sounded like a better deal than what I had. Yet I admired Rich so much that I just couldn't come right out and admit to being a prostitute.

He must have been reading my thoughts. "Lori," he said kindly, "you probably won't admit to me who you really are, but there's Someone who knows all about you—even from before you were born. . . ."

That got to me. Did God know about me while my mother was trying to miscarry? Could that really be true?

"I know the Lord brought you here for a purpose," Rich continued, "and that purpose was not immorality. That purpose was so you could meet Jesus. He loves you so much, Lori, that He arranged for you to be here on this particular weekend so you could hear the girls from the Walter Hoving Home. Their testimonies, I'm sure, told about the kind of life you know something about. I couldn't help but notice your wrists, Lori." Involuntarily I stuck my hands behind my back.

"I don't know whether or not you've ever had a walk with the Lord, but this would be a beautiful time to give your heart to Jesus and get straightened out. Jesus really loves you, Lori—I mean He *really* does."

Any contrived anger I had felt completely drained from me now. My heart felt like wax, and a lump came into my throat. I slowly bowed my head and stared at the ground. Rich slid over close and put his strong arm around me.

Tears flowed as I buried my head in his chest. He just let me cry for a few minutes, tenderly patting my arm every now and then. Finally he pulled out his handkerchief and gently wiped away the tears and kissed my cheek.

I squeezed him tighter and snuggled my cheek against his. I kept on crying, and he kept wiping my tears.

For a fleeting second that ten thousand dollars flitted across my brain, but I had lost my lust. I wanted real love, pure love, the kind Rich had.

It seemed a long time that we sat there while I cried my eyes out, but finally I took a deep breath and decided to let it all hang out.

"Rich, I've lied to you. I've tried to entice you. And I did it all for money. Your uncle promised me five thousand dollars if I could get you into bed with me. My pimp was to get another five thousand dollars. I've mistreated you for the sake of money. It was so wrong, Rich. I feel so cheap." The tears started again.

"Oh, Lori, no problem," Rich replied as he dabbed at my cheeks. "I just thank God that He knew what I needed and that His grace was sufficient for me to withstand your temptation.

"But I'll have to admit one thing. When we were watching television that first night, I started to get excited. I was really glad Uncle George came in. It gave me time to come to my senses, and I dropped to my knees to ask God to cool me down. You see, Lori, there's something about you I really like. Deep down inside you have something really good and beautiful."

"Oh, Rich, you're so loving and so kind. I just wish I could be like you. If only there was—"

Suddenly I heard footsteps approaching and jumped up. "Hey, you two," Mr. Witmore called. "Are you out here somewhere?"

Then he spotted us. "What's going on, anyway? I heard some yelling and screaming, and I thought I'd better investigate."

What was I going to tell him? I couldn't blow Rich's cover. I answered, "Mr. Witmore, I just don't know what I'm going to do with this nephew of yours. He quoted a verse from the Bible, and that started it. We got into this big argument, and I'm not the quiet kind when I argue!"

"That's okay, Lori. I know what you're talking about, but Rich is really a good guy, just a little misdirected, that's all."

"I'll agree with you on that. He is a fantastic guy, but too religious, if you know what I mean."

Mr. Witmore smiled at me and whispered, "Don't take it too hard, Lori. Others have tried and failed. That Rich—he's like the Rock of Gibraltar."

I knew that Rich must have overheard that and known exactly what Mr. Witmore was talking about. But did Mr. Witmore know that Rich knew?

"Well, I hate to break up this pleasant little meeting," Mr. Witmore went on, "but a couple of your friends are here from the city to get you, Lori."

Two guys? Strange. Only Lawrence knew I was here. Could it be those two policemen? But how would they have found me?

When we walked into the main house, I got the shock of my life. There stood Amos and Randy!

"Well, hello there, Lori," Amos said in a sickenly sweet voice. "How's my little friend? I understand you've been having a little weekend vacation out here. I think it's wonderful of your boss to let you get a little rest and relaxation!"

How was I going to get out of this one? I couldn't outrun Amos. I wanted to rush to Rich's strong arms for safety. But knowing these two, they probably had guns with them, and they would stop at nothing to get me. I couldn't risk letting anything happen to Rich.

"Oh, Amos, it's been fantastic around here," I answered. "I think I'll just spend the rest of my life out here."

"Well, I hate to disappoint you, but your boss asked Randy and me to come and pick you up. So here we are, and it's time to go—if you know what I mean."

I knew. "Okay, Amos. Fine. Let me go upstairs and pack."

As I started up the stairs, Amos said, "If you don't mind, folks, maybe I'd just better go along with Lori—in case she needs help with her suitcase. A person could easily get lost in a big house like this!" He laughed, and so did Randy. The other two didn't. I think they knew what was up.

Amos trailed me up the stairs. I tried to ignore him as I threw my things into my overnight case. But that rape was still burning in my mind. If I somehow could get revenge! But why would Lawrence send these two for me? It didn't make any sense.

As I started toward the stairs again, Amos fell in step behind me. "Okay, Lori, one false move, and I'll blow your brains out. Randy's got the other two covered downstairs. If you come along without any problems, you won't get hurt. But if you don't, you and your rich friends will be in big trouble. Lawrence wants to see you."

Back in the living room I told Rich and Mr. Witmore good-bye and thanked them for the fabulous weekend. I threw my arms around Rich and felt myself starting to cry again. I bit my tongue. I didn't want anyone to know how I felt about him.

Amos pushed me into the backseat of their car and got in with me. Randy drove. I waved good-bye to Rich. There stood my Prince Charming, but even he couldn't rescue me from the clutches of these two thugs. This was the end. If only I could have escaped from this kind of life. But it was too late now.

Nobody said anything as we drove toward the city. They took me right to Lawrence's apartment. I guess that surprised me. Why were they working for him?

The first thing Lawrence said was, "Well, did you succeed?"

"Lawrence, you would never believe what I ran into. This nephew really is a religious nut. He spent the whole time trying to convert me. I had absolutely no more of a chance of getting that guy than the man in the moon. He was impossible."

"Lori, I thought you were better than that. I was really counting on you. Look, you're young, beautiful, and have a great body. You mean with all that you couldn't get that kid into bed with you?"

"I'm telling you, Lawrence, there was absolutely no way. But I think he likes me. He told me he did. So I'll tell you what. Why don't you arrange for me to go up there again next weekend? I think the second time around will do it!"

As I said it, I knew that would be my way out. Before, I couldn't think of anywhere I could go if I got away from Lawrence. Now I knew there was a place—the Walter Hoving Home. Rich would take me there.

"Nice try," Lawrence said, bringing me back to reality, "but it won't work. Besides, I've got some johns already lined up for you. They're asking for you. You're becoming more valuable all the time! In fact, I've expanded my business because of you. Amos and Randy are working for me, now. They'll be watching over you and helping you!"

I looked at those two oxen and still felt rage for what they had done to me. If I ever got the chance....

True to his word, Lawrence had fixed me up with a couple of men that evening. But then it was right back to the street, only this time it was different: everywhere I went, Amos and Randy tailed me.

As I stood on the corner hustling, I made up my mind that I was going to get out of this mess—how, I didn't know.

The following Friday night was extremely busy around Times Square. Amos had lined up several guys for me. Every time I went to a hotel room, the experience was almost unbearable.

It was about one o'clock in the morning when a young man walked by me on the street. He smiled, and I thought, *Boy, here's a quick one!* I walked up and said, "Want to have a good time?"

He smiled again. "What do you mean?"

"You know, go out—like you and me, to a nice hotel room."

"Sounds like a great idea," he answered. "In fact, I have one in mind. Why don't you come with me?"

He looked so clean-cut and safe—and he was kind of good-looking. Not as good-looking as Rich, of course, but attractive. I knew Amos and Randy would be close by, so I figured I had nothing to lose. I fell in step beside him as we started up Eighth Avenue.

"I hope you don't mind," he said, "but we have a few blocks to walk."

"Well, that all depends. How much are you going to pay me?"

He smiled. "Let's just leave it at this, young lady; it will be more than worth your time."

I knew I should bargain with him now. But he looked so clean-cut. I'd wait until I got to his room.

Up to Fifty-fourth Street. Then toward Ninth

Avenue. Hey, the best hotels were the other way. Only a few run-down apartment houses were this way. My heart beat faster.

Past Ninth Avenue toward Tenth.

"Sir, you mentioned a hotel room. I don't think there are any hotels in this direction, are there?"

He laughed. "Lori, I'll just take you to the middle of the block, and then we'll circle back. Okay?"

How did he know my name? I'd never seen him before. Did somebody recommend me?

"How'd you know who I was?"

"Now don't worry. A guy pointed you out to me."

In the middle of the block I noticed a man sitting in a car. Oh, no! Not again! But before I had a chance to even think of screaming, this young kid had thrown his coat over my head, grabbed my arms, and pushed me into the car.

"I got her! Take off!" he shouted to the driver.

I tried kicking and screaming. No use. He was sitting on top of me to hold me down. My heart raced wildly as the car jerked away from the curb. I just knew where we were headed—toward Fifty-eighth Street and the docks.

I couldn't live through another rape!

FOURTEEN

Kidnapped! These dudes must have rape in mind. They wouldn't hold a prostitute for ransom, would they? Or were they in the business and were taking me to another city?

At this rate, I won't live to tell about it! my mind echoed. That coat over me was smothering me. I couldn't scream or kick. That kid sure was powerful!

Then I heard a car behind us honking wildly. Someone shouted, "Stop! Stop! Police!"

That voice—I knew it. That accent. Yes, it was Amos! He'd seen what had happened and was trying to rescue me.

Rescue! That was a laugh. I didn't know which would be worse: Amos or these maniacs. What a choice! What a picture of my life—always from bad to worse. It was too bad I hadn't tried harder in some of those suicide attempts.

Then the shooting started. *Amos must be firing at us.* But there was no sound from our car. Right away I stopped kicking and slithered down as far as I could get.

We squealed around a corner. That sent me

slamming against the door. The kid hugged me really close—almost as though he was trying to protect me. *Am I that valuable a piece of property?*

Tires squealed as we rounded another corner. Then another. And another. No more shots! Had he shaken Amos? I didn't know whether to laugh or cry!

After what seemed like an eternity the car slowed down. The driver called back, "I think we made it, Jeff."

That voice! I recognized it, too. *Was it—could it be....*

Then Jeff pulled his coat away. I jumped, expecting him to grab at me. He just settled back and smiled.

"Hi, Lori!" the driver said.

I wheeled around toward him. No wonder I recognized that voice! "Rich Witmore! What on earth do you think you're doing?"

"I have just committed my first kidnapping, and what a prize I came up with!"

I lunged forward and threw my arms around him. I squeezed his neck and kissed his cheek. No worries now! I was safe!

"Wow, Rich, that was close!" Jeff said. "When that cop started firing, I thought it was the end."

"You and me, both," I said. "But for your information, that was no cop. That was Amos—the guy who was supposed to be watching out for me."

"Amos?" Rich asked. "That dude who picked you up at Uncle George's last week?"

"That's the same turkey. He's no closer to being a cop than I am to being president of the United States."

"Well, thank God we got you this far," Rich said.

"This far? What do you two guys have in mind?"

Rich put his arm on the back of the seat so he could

turn and face me once in a while, and still watch where he was driving. I rested my chin lightly on his arm.

"Let me fill you in on what's happened," he began. "Do you remember Raquel? Well, I was right. She was a prostitute. My uncle kept trying to hire her, and she stayed out there all week. But I guess they never could come to terms, and she demanded to be taken back to town—right away. Uncle asked me if I would mind taking her in. I guess Raquel was threatening to blow his cover, and he got nervous. He also found out that I knew what he was up to. He didn't want the chauffeur to drive her in. Anyway, Jeff had been visiting me, so I got him to come along. I figured it would look better than for me to be driving alone with Raquel.

"Well, Lori, all week long I couldn't get you out of my mind. I've really been praying for you. After we let Raquel out, we cruised around Times Square for a while, and I told Jeff about you."

"Who's Jeff?" I asked.

"Forgive me. My partner in crime is seated next to you—Jeff Beardsley. He's an old college chum I met in Inter-Varsity. He and his wife live in Connecticut and go to my church. His wife went to visit her folks this weekend, and he came up to spend some time with me."

"Okay, so what happened?"

"Well, as we were cruising around Times Square, I spotted you on a corner. I knew I couldn't go up to you myself. I figured your pimp was on the lookout for you. So I asked Jeff to proposition you, and we worked out this kidnapping scheme."

He laughed as he thought about it! The crazy guys. They could easily have gotten themselves killed!

"When we saw you, Lori," Jeff said, "we just knew

that God had answered our prayers. And we thought of the kidnapping scheme so that if you did escape, you could tell your pimp that someone had tried to kidnap you—and you wouldn't be in trouble. At least, it would have given you a way out."

"And one other thing, Lori," Rich interrupted. "I've got something in mind I'd like for you to do. But if you say no, you can still go back to your pimp and say you were kidnapped. You've got a legitimate excuse."

I still didn't know why these two had cooked up this scheme—certainly not for me to join his uncle's house of prostitution. That sure didn't add up.

"Lori," Rich went on, "I really felt as though God was speaking to you last weekend. I even think you may have tried to get out of prostitution—if we hadn't been interrupted in our conversation by your so-called friends. And I honestly believe that God let us find you tonight.

"Here's what it all adds up to. Jeff and I are willing to drive you up to the Walter Hoving Home right now, Lori. There you can receive loving care and understanding. Most of all, you can come to know Jesus and learn to live for Him. It will be a life to be proud of and to enjoy."

The whole thing almost blew my mind. Could God be so interested in me that, almost as soon as I thought of a way out of my mess, He provided it for me? Did He really have His hand in tonight's circumstances?

I sat there in silence, trying to comprehend what was happening and wondering if it were all a dream. Rich slowed and pulled to the curb.

"My neck is getting stiff from turning around so much. Lori, would you mind sitting up here with me? Maybe we can talk a little bit more."

Would I mind? The car had barely stopped before I

was out and back in again! Rich gently took my hand.

We headed north on FDR Drive. Once again my life flashed before me—the separation from my family, the suicide attempts, the heartless life of a prostitute. I wanted to shout, "Yes, Rich! Please take me away from my past! Take me to the Walter Hoving Home, now!"

But I couldn't.

"Lori, let me say something else before you tell me yes or no. In decisions such as this, there's a Bible verse the Lord often reminds me of. It says, 'For we wrestle not against flesh and blood, but against principalities, against powers, against the rulers of the darkness. . . .' You see, Lori, the devil is trying to persuade you against what I'm suggesting. There's a battle going on in your heart between good and evil. But if you decide for Jesus, He's made plans for you that are for your good. I promise you, you won't be sorry!"

I know it should have been easy, but it was one of the most difficult things I have ever said: "Rich, I've been thinking about you and what you said to me all week long. Please take me up there. I can't say I want to go, but I know I ought to."

No sooner were the words out than Rich slipped his arm around me and squeezed. I felt so secure in his arms. Maybe everything was going to be okay!

Rich said it was only about an hour's drive up to Garrison. But would they take me at this time of night?

The farther we got from Times Square, the farther I seemed to be from all the evil and hell of my life. The closer we got to Garrison, the more peace I experienced.

I put my head on Rich's shoulder and listened while he and Jeff told me about the home and its program. Rich said that the girls go to classes from eight in the morning until two in the afternoon. Then came work.

"The home takes the Bible teachings and applies them to life," Jeff said.

"Yes, and you're going to love the staff," Rich chimed in, "especially the Reverend and Mrs. Benton. The girls call him Brother B and her Mom B. They're in charge of the home. I've met them, and they seem like super, fine people."

It was rather dark as we started up the driveway of the home. Excitement shot through me. *We're really here!* The car lights showed enough that I could see it wās absolutely beautiful. Then we came to the three-story English Tudor mansion. Wow! God must be good to provide a place such as this for me!

A rather sleepy Mom B answered our persistent ringing of the door bell. She studied Rich and then apparently remembered him from his earlier visit there. She looked at me, and I guess she must have put the whole thing together. Before I knew what was happening, she threw her arms around me and drew me close. "Oh, what a beautiful girl!" she exclaimed. "I just can't help loving you girls. You look so sweet!"

It felt good to have someone care about me. Rich, Jeff, and now this lady. I knew I'd get along well with Mom B.

She invited us into the living room and motioned for us to sit down. One of the girls came to see what was happening and, without being asked, brought us some coffee.

My story spilled out. They all listened sympathetically. Because it was so late, Mom B suggested we wait until morning to fill out the necessary forms. Jeff kept saying they had to leave, and Rich kept finding excuses to stay longer. Jeff finally got the four of us out onto the porch. Then Rich took my hand and pulled me toward the car. I sensed he wanted to say something to me privately.

As we got to his car, he turned me around to face him. "Lori, I can't tell you how happy I am because of your decision. God really worked a miracle so that you could come here. I guess you know that. As you learn to walk with Him, your life is going to be so different."

"Rich, it's happening already. There is such a beautiful spirit of peace in this place. This is where I should be." I reached over and took his hand. "Rich, if you hadn't prayed and rescued me tonight, do you know where I'd be right now?"

He smiled.

"Rich, I would still be in that hellhole—and with no hope! I owe my life to you, Rich."

"The credit all belongs to the Lord, Lori. He's the One who really loves you and is watching out for you. But I want you to know something else. What I did tonight I wouldn't do for just any girl. You're *really* special!"

That beautiful smile! I couldn't get over it. I tried to answer, but the words wouldn't come. But the tears did.

"Lori, I'll always remember you." Then I felt his arms slip around me. He drew me close and kissed me. I squeezed, too. This felt so good. So pure.

Then I heard footsteps. Mom B saw us and laughed. "Just like my husband and me. Any chance I get, I always grab him for a quick kiss!" We all laughed. That Mom B really had a sense of humor.

"I'll check tomorrow and see how you're doing," Rich said as he got into the car. "I just know everything will be different from now on!"

I knew it, too. Maybe destiny had finally caught up with me.

I watched until his car disappeared down the long driveway, then we went back into the house. One of the girls showed me to my bedroom. It was so pretty and feminine. And in no time at all I was fast asleep—but maybe not fast enough because that was one of the shortest nights I remember. We had breakfast at 7:00 A.M.!

That day my head was in a spin. So many people to meet. Everything so different. But I loved every minute of it.

After supper Mom B took me down to the prayer room and explained to me from the Bible how to be saved. She made it so clear. She said I needed to confess my sins to Jesus and by faith believe that He forgave them. She told me again how He had died on the cross to pay the debt of my sin.

She showed me Roman 10:9, 10 in the Bible: "If thou shalt confess with thy mouth the Lord Jesus, and shalt believe in thine heart that God hath raised him from the dead, thou shalt be saved. For with the heart man believeth unto righteousness; and with the mouth confession is made unto salvation."

Well, I was ready. She had me repeat a prayer after her, asking Jesus to forgive my sins and take over my life. It was so simple! I wondered why no one had ever told me before!

Then Mom B told me the importance of daily Bible reading and prayer—spiritual food to nourish my spiritual life, she said. This way I could learn how Jesus wanted me to live. This was called applying the Bible to everyday living.

After I was at the home for three months, I learned a difficult lesson. I hadn't contacted my family. Yet I knew that now that I was a Christian, one of my concerns would be my family. That's how Jesus wanted it to work. But what could I tell them?

I just didn't have the courage to call my family, so Mom B did. She let them know where I was and that I was safe. They seemed relieved, she said. And I found out that Mom was back home.

Two months later I got my first pass. I knew I should go home, but I didn't want to face my family alone, so Mom B offered to go with me. I couldn't get over the kindness of that woman!

The morning we were to leave I was so nervous— and really cranky, the girls told me later. But they were patient with me. They'd been through the same kind of thing!

Mom B had called ahead, so Mom, Dad, and Peggy were all waiting for me when we arrived. They couldn't believe all that had happened to me since they had last seen me, especially the religion part of it. Mom B did her best to explain it.

After we had been there a couple of hours, I asked my folks to come into the bedroom with me. I asked them to forgive me for not being the daughter I was supposed to be. I had missed God's plan, I told them, but I was on the right track now. You should have seen their surprise when I asked them to forgive me! They couldn't get over it! All Dad would say was that I surely was different.

I pressed the question. Then both of my parents said they forgave me. I felt as though a great weight had been lifted from me.

Before I left, I asked the three of them to visit me in Garrison. They said they would try.

Two weeks later, on a Sunday afternoon, I was sitting in the living room, reading. Then the front door

opened, and there stood Mom, Dad, and Peggy! I
squealed with delight and threw my arms around them.
They backed up a little. They weren't used to the new
me, yet!

I introduced them to the other girls and showed them
around. They couldn't get over everything. They even
agreed to stay for our evening service.

I knew God was getting through to them. Mom B
knew it, too. She asked them to go to the prayer room
with her. Would you believe what happened? Right!
Mom and Dad and Peggy all received Jesus as their
Saviour! They said they wanted whatever had made
such a difference in me. I was thrilled beyond words!
We were a Christian family, now!

Oh, yes, I had another visitor from time to
time—Rich. And every time he came, he stayed longer
and longer. I knew I was falling in love. But how did he
feel about me? After all, he knew what kind of a girl I
had been. It's one thing to gallantly rescue a fallen girl,
but to marry her?

Near the end of my year at the home, Brother B
talked to me about my future. I made plans to go to
Evangel College in Missouri. Many of the girls from the
home had gone to that Christian college, he said. Others
went to Bible school, and still others went back to their
families.

Graduation night was beautiful. My family came. So
did Rich. I felt so proud to receive my graduation
certificate. It was the first time I had ever completed
something in my life! And the Lord helped me do it.

I went home with my folks for a few months before
college. We were so happy as a family with faith in
Christ. As Brother B had suggested, they had been
attending Calvary Tabernacle. Years ago, when the

girls' home was in New York City, that had been their home church. "Pastor Crandall is a great preacher," Brother B had told them. "He'll help you grow in the Lord."

I enjoyed the service, but I had something else to look forward to on weekends—Rich. He always drove over, and we'd go to church together. Sometimes he'd take me to a Christian concert or to a nice place to eat. We'd talk and get to know each other better.

Then one night it happened. We had headed north on the Palisades Parkway. About five miles up there was a place to turn off the main road and look over the lights of the city. As we sat there, Rich drew me up close and kissed me. Then he asked, "Lori, will you marry me?"

Bells rang! Rockets lit the sky! I threw my arms around him and sighed, "Oh, yes! Yes! Any time you're ready, I'm ready!"

He squeezed me tightly, and we both giggled in ecstacy.

"Lori, you've made me the happiest man alive!" he exclaimed. "I've been in love with you for some time now, and God has worked it out for us. This is so beautiful." I tried to agree, but he smothered me with kisses.

Well, Rich and I did get married soon after that. I never did get to college, but the Lord is teaching me to be the Christian wife I ought to be. Maybe someday I'll get a chance to take some college training.

Rich, of course, is very prominent in his uncle's business.

Oh, yes, I must tell you about Uncle George. He gave up that house of prostitution. He almost got killed over it and decided it wasn't worth the risk.

We're still praying that he will come to know Jesus as

his Saviour. Oh, yes! Would you believe that, with a twinkle in his eye, he gave us five thousand dollars for a wedding gift?

I worried a little about Rich and my past. I'm sure he's thought about it, but never once has he brought it up. He's a real prince. He talks about the present and the future. He said that's the way Jesus is. He forgives our past and helps us now and in the future. Rich said he wanted to be like Jesus. What a man!

The two of us began a special ministry on weekends. Rich said he could appeal to the "up and outer." I told about the other side—the "down and outer." Our ministry has really caught on. Hundreds of people call us for help.

The two of us really make a beautiful combination. That's the way Jesus is. He died not only to save the bad but also the good. As the Bible says, "*All* have sinned, and come short of the glory of God" (*see* Romans 3:23).

How about you? You can be a very good person and still need Jesus. Maybe you're like Rich—you seem to have it all together, but you still need a Saviour.

Or maybe you're like me. You've hit the bottom.

Maybe you're like me in another way—you've been thinking seriously of suicide. Believe me, that's not the way out.

Will you let me give you some help? Even since I've become a Christian, I have some difficult days, and those thoughts come back. But I've learned to control them. Here's how:

I've told myself those depressing thoughts won't stay forever, and, sure enough, they don't. But when they come around, I read more than ever from God's Word and I pray. God helps me.

There is something else I've learned from counseling potential suicides: whenever they've shared these